CONTINUUM

Continuum: Collected Stories of Space and Time is the third book by Luke Herzog and his first collection of short stories and novellas. Luke published his first novel, ***Dragon Valley,*** while he was in elementary school and completed his second novel, ***Griffin Blade and the Bronze Finger,*** as a middle schooler. He wrote the tales compiled in Continuum during his first three years in high school. In 2018, Luke was selected as a writing finalist by the National YoungArts Foundation, one of 20 students nationwide who received the honor. He was also awarded a Scholastic Art & Writing gold medal, as well as a National Council of Teachers of English (NCTE) Achievement Award in Writing. Luke lives in California with his family and his dog, Pippin, named after J.R.R. Tolkien's mischievous hobbit. For more information, visit LukeHerzog.com.

You see things, and you say "Why?"
But I dream things that never were, and I say "Why not?"

–George Bernard Shaw

WHY NOT BOOKS

Pacific Grove, California | www.WhyNotBooks.com

Why Not Books is dedicated to producing good books and good karma. Toward that end, we partner each title with a charitable organization and donate a portion of proceeds to the cause. The nonprofit partner for this book is Monterey County Reads, which is dedicated to providing children with the tools they need to achieve happy and productive lives. The program uses literacy as a means to avoid poverty by pairing young students with volunteer readers at elementary schools through-out California's Monterey County.

CONTINUUM

COLLECTED STORIES
OF SPACE AND TIME

LUKE HERZOG

www.whynotbooks.com
www.lukeherzog.com

ISBN: 978-0-9978808-4-7
Library of Congress Control Number: 2018905680
First Edition: August 2018
Printed in the United States of America

Cover and interior design and layout by Tessa Avila

To my grandparents,
who have always made space and time for me

CONTENTS

FISHBOWL

Expedition Roster

EXPEDITION 144:

Varun Duvvur (India)—Commander
Gabriel Florez (United States)—First Officer
Clifford "Red" Kaznach (Russia)—Second Officer

EXPEDITION 145:

Lesedi Naidoo (South Africa)—Commander
Dimitri Sadakov (Russia)—First Officer
David Dixon (United States)—Second Officer

EXPEDITION 146:

Yamato Sho (Japan)—Commander
Noah Abrams (United States)—First Officer
Eva Topfsky (Russia)—Second Officer

PART ONE

Unanchored

"We may brave human laws, but we cannot resist natural ones."

—Jules Verne
20,000 Leagues Under the Sea

F or a week, the mushroom clouds left red dots on the astronaut's eyes—bloody phantoms dancing in his vision, taunting him. Closing his lids offered no respite from the torment. It had been four days since the bombings stopped, but the fires raged on. Abrams knew it wasn't healthy, taking every opportunity to spare a glance at the destruction below. But he couldn't look away. He was determined to bear witness to man's darkest hours. It was the least he could do, for the guilt was all-consuming. Floating above, watching Armageddon from the safety of their little palace in the sky. Abrams felt his stomach twist.

He was no less fascinated by his colleagues, 230 miles above the worst case scenario. Each astronaut coped differently. Topfsky had retreated into her calculations, murmuring about fallout and wind patterns. She hunched over hastily ripped notebook paper so filled with equations and notations that she'd begun scribbling over previous ones. Discarded pages spiraled around her now, as if she was the star in her own solar system. Florez's diet had become irregular, to say the least. Caring too little to add water to powdered coffee and Kool-Aid, he scarfed them down dry—a nebulous cloud of brown and purple dust plastered to his face and followed him about. Even Dixon's incessant toothy grin had long since been supplanted by a forlorn smile and furrowed brow, his light humor having descended into darkness and cynicism.

They passed over the half of the planet cloaked in shadow. The fires were more distinct against the black backdrop, flickering like torch bugs on a warm summer night.

Abrams was stirred by the sound of conversation, an almost alien concept as the hours passed, usually reserved for discussion of raw data and bleak hypotheticals. The buzz of consoles and the perpetual scratch of pencil lead had become white noise during their dark vigil for the human race.

"Ya spelled apocalypse wrong, darlin'," chided Dixon. The towering Texan hovered parallel to the engineer, face-to-face but upside-down. His goatee and shaved head made him look right-side up. Topfsky's eyes flickered, then she continued her scribbling.

"So I did. What's it to you?"

He shrugged. "Ain't the end of the world." Dixon smiled weakly. Topfsky looked disgusted.

"What are you working on?" Abrams turned his attention from the window and pushed against a bulkhead, launching himself toward the other two.

Topfsky sighed. "I'm writing an account of all that's occurred. The better question is—why aren't you?" Abrams's nose twitched. "What if ours is the only record to survive? Future historians might depend on our account... It might be all they have to go on."

Dixon raised an eyebrow. "Never had ya figured as a writer, Topfsky."

"Why so surprised?"

"Just always thought you wrote in binary."

She pushed him away, enough to send him floating backwards, and tugged a strand of hair behind her ear. "Jackass..."

Red appeared beside her, scratching at his chin and rolling his eyes as the Texan flailed for a handhold. The man's actual name was Clifford Kaznach. Dixon was responsible for the nickname—a not-so-subtle dig at Kaznach's Communist connections, though the man-child insisted he was referencing *Clifford, the Big Red Dog*. Nevertheless, it caught on. Abrams suspected that even the Russian had taken a liking to it.

"God, I'd like to sew his mouth shut," Red whispered in flawless English. He nodded toward the view of the destruction below. "And I wish we could draw the blinds, too, you know?"

No, I don't, thought Abrams. "Yeah."

"So I was just talking to Duvvur," Red continued.

"Does the commander want another meeting?" Once the bombings had ceased, Commander Duvvur had called for a vote. Stay or go. Remain in orbit and hope rations—and the station itself—hold out long enough for a safe return, or attempt a landing on a toxic world. They had long since lost contact with Earth; the choice was theirs and theirs alone. For all they knew, the planet was, too. The debate was long and intense. Opinions were evenly split. In the end, Duvvur cast the deciding vote. They would stay.

Red had been in the minority. *What's the first thing you do when you hear your house is on fire? You run home,* he had reasoned. But the blaze was only spreading. "No, the commander doesn't want a meeting, but..."

Abrams eyed Topfsky. She *appeared* thoroughly immersed in her writings. Abrams knew her tricks well enough by now. "The aft." Red agreed.

¤

By now, the aft was in disarray. The sour smell of unwashed men and sudden indifference blanketed everything. Free-floating materials nestled in every nook and cranny. Crumpled papers and food crumbs, even wandering wrappers and packaging, drifted alongside the two sleeping bags affixed to the walls. Red and Florez spent a lot of time here. Years of training and a mission together had even left their disorganization symbiotic.

In the room's corner, Dixon had stashed a contribution—a golf club, a shiny pitching wedge in honor of the swings Alan Shepard attempted on the lunar surface over half a century earlier.

Several scattered novels, Red's favorites, glided throughout the compartment like circling vultures. Abrams snatched a book floating between a paperback edition of *The Hunt for Red October* and a tattered Agatha Christie thriller.

"*From the Earth to the Moon*," he read.

Red moved closer. "You know what Jules Verne did, right? You know how the first three men got to the moon?" Abrams shook his head. Red took the book from his hands. "I'll have to lend it to you sometime."

"So what's the problem?" Abrams asked.

"Rations."

"I know, I know. We've gone over this a dozen times. Nine crew, only supposed to be six at a time." The crew of Expedition 146—Abrams, Topfsky, and Sho—had arrived only three days before the first bomb fell. During this transitional phase, Expedition 144 hadn't yet departed. The end of the world had been poorly timed. "We figured we're good for about six months. By then..."

"But that's if all goes well. Sadakov and I went over the math again. The numbers are worse than we feared. What we didn't take into account was the real possibility of the station's systems deteriorating. Or space junk. If satellites start failing at an alarming rate—there's already enough debris in orbit, now it's going to increase exponentially. If we can't avoid it..."

"Lots of ifs."

"I'm well aware. If bad weather hadn't delayed your expedition's launch. If final diagnostic tests hadn't brought up that glitch. If I hadn't been so damn sentimental as to insist on one more sunrise from space..." Red glanced down at the 144 insignia on his breast pocket. "I can't help but feel we've overstayed our welcome."

"You're not blaming yourself—"

"You would have a better shot at survival."

"And you would be an ash heap."

Red rubbed his temples. "Six months at *most*, Abrams. And that's while rationing to the extreme. That means hunger for half a year. And that's if orbital decay doesn't screw us first."

"We'll find a way. The bombings seem to be over. We'll establish contact again, you'll see. Surely someone will remember we're still up here, eh?" Abrams hoped he sounded sincere.

¤

It sounded like a thunderclap. And Abrams was blasted away from the space station, barreling into the void. He found himself drifting aimlessly in the vacuum, his consciousness retreating until he saw the station for what it was—a rogue speck of dust silhouetted against an ashen world. Insignificant. Inconsequential.

Like an arrow shot into oblivion, his journey continued. Soon his planet was left behind. He shivered as he shed Sol's familiar cradle. Warmth was a force unknown in the spaces between the stars. Then the stars themselves became blurs of light. Glancing behind, he watched a streak of white brilliance— the galaxy's rim—dim and then disappear. He flew on, plunged into absolute darkness, all direction lost. A sickeningly sweet scent filled his nostrils. Sweet as pine sap, yet metallic like a freshly minted coin. All was black. Only the scent lingered...

Abrams sniffed. *What the hell?* He blinked his eyes open. He smelled blood.

He fumbled to loosen the straps that held him to his bed. His sleeping compartment was closest to the botany lab, and as he rounded the corner, he stopped short. Meandering red ribbons weaved between the ferns and stalks like a lazy tropical river. And the delta—a gaping wound, a lifeless body.

"Commander. . ." Duvvur's sprawled corpse, arms splayed, hovered in the room's center, a morbid marionette. The commander's cool intensity had vanished in death. His piercing brown eyes were dull, muddy pools. His wire-rimmed glasses hovered among quivering crimson globules.

Abrams's tongue felt swollen, too large for his mouth. The lab began to sway and undulate. Suddenly he was back in the torturous human centrifuge during astronaut training, the acceleration draining the blood from his head. Just like in Houston, he nearly blacked out.

He blinked himself steady and forced his eyes to take in the gruesome scene in its entirety. "Jesus..." Something had to be done. For a moment, he hovered over the body. And then...

"Naidoo!" Abrams's heart boomed in his ears. "Someone find Naidoo! Quick, dammit!"

One at a time, the crew groggily filtered in, each jolted into alertness by the grotesque form of their commander. Topfsky stifled a scream. Florez turned green. Sadakov grabbed at the silver cross around his neck. Naidoo arrived last.

"Oh my god... Out of the way, out of the way! Make room." She forced herself through the cluster of astronauts. The medic had seen many horrific wartime injuries in her career, but even her trained doctor's calm wavered. She hesitated briefly before coming forward to examine the body. Naidoo swallowed. Her poised demeanor could not mask the fear in her voice. "A bullet wound. Straight through the skull." The crew was silent.

Dixon ran his fingers across his stubbled scalp. "Sonofabitch has gone an' killed himself."

"But Duvvur... He wouldn't..." Florez diverted his eyes from the floating corpse. He looked like he was about to belch up a stomach-full of powdered coffee. "He was always steady. Even when the bombs started to fall."

Topfsky shook her head. "That could bring anyone to the breaking point." Another silence.

"Then where is the gun?" Sho's voice was a deep baritone, ominous as a storm cloud. The little Japanese man looked down, as if guilty for having made the discovery. The astronauts scanned the carnage, each coming to the same conclusion. There was no firearm to be found amid the bloody rivulets.

Their faces darkened. Dixon, reliably verbal, said aloud what the crew was considering. "If he shot himself, the gun'd be floatin' around here someplace..."

"Unless..." Abrams ventured, trailing off. "Unless it wasn't suicide." Abrams winced right after the words left his lips. The room erupted in a chorus of curses and protests.

Naidoo's declaration cut through it all. "A crew member is *dead*!" The din ground to a halt. "Stop bickering and treat him with the same respect you gave him in life."

"Well what do we do now? What's the procedure?" asked Topfsky. Tears formed in her eyes.

Naidoo exhaled. "We handle the most immediate issues first, then consider the greater implications. I want a suit brought down from the joint airlock. Sho?"

Sho nodded. "Sadakov, Red." He gestured at them to follow, and they filtered out.

Naidoo turned to Abrams. "You know where the Contaminated Cleanup Kits are, right? Take Florez and Topfsky. I'll see to it that the commander is safely removed. You three will be charged with cleaning and decontaminating the lab."

"And me?" Dixon scanned the room.

"You're sending NASA a message. Say there has been a Loss of Crew, cause of death—gun wound."

"Commander, I'm trained specifically to operate onboard communications..." Abrams started.

"Dixon will do."

The Texan balked. "But we don't know if NASA even exists anymore."

"I don't care if you are talking to a pile of rubble. We're doing this by the book, Dixon." The Texan's lip curled, but he did as he was told.

¤

PSYCHOLOGICAL EVALUATION

Expedition 145
Subject: David Dixon
Born: 10/16/95; Houston, Texas

Subject refused to conduct himself in a serious manner during much of the psychological testing phase. Subtle jabs and sarcastic remarks peppered Lt. Dixon's evaluation, of which he made a mockery. What little light could be shed on Subject's mental state was derived not from official procedure, but instead his demeanor during questioning. Responses indicate a natural tendency to resist authority, and Subject's restlessness and his apparent inability to focus are symptomatic of ADHD.

Included are excerpts of key exchanges.

TIMESTAMP—10:37 AM

MAGNUS: Thank you for agreeing to speak with us, Lieutenant Dixon. If you're willing, we'd like to run a few simple psychological tests.

DIXON: Sure thing, Doc.

METAXA: I'm going to hold up a blank sheet of paper. We'd like you to tell us what you see—is there a problem, Lieutenant?

DIXON: [stifles laughter] No sir. It's just—

METAXA: —Yes?—

DIXON: Just a funny concept, is all.

METAXA: Lieutenant Dixon, you are one of the candidates who could be selected to essentially share an orbiting apartment with five other individuals for half a year. I assure you, your mental health is no laughing matter.

DIXON: [smiles] Of course. My bad, please go on.

METAXA: Very well. [holds up blank piece of paper] What do you see?

DIXON: What do I see?

METAXA: [nods]

DIXON: [after thirty seconds of intense reflection] I... I can't do it.

MAGNUS: [leans forward, pen at the ready] Why not?

DIXON: You're holding it upside-down.

TIMESTAMP—11:16 AM

METAXA: [reads from document on table] Decorated air force pilot, years of engineering experience, top of your class at MIT...

MAGNUS: How do you feel about that, being top of your class?

DIXON: [shrugs] It's just rocket science.

MAGNUS: So, why an astronaut?

DIXON: Sealed up like a sardine and shipped into space?

MAGNUS: Well, yes.

DIXON: Now that you ask... Ya see, all my life I'd heard the phrase "what goes up must come down," right? So I figured I'd stick it to Newton, and get a little stargazing in while I was at it. Two birds with one stone an' all that.

METAXA: Most people in your position say something about "scientific advancement" or "pushing boundaries..."

DIXON: Now those folks are either lyin' or kiddin' themselves. We're all selfish, whether we admit it or not. Space is groovy, NASA's givin' out roundtrip passes. That's all there is to it.

MAGNUS: Well your... honesty, is appreciated.

DIXON: [pantomimes tipping his hat]

METAXA: You grew up in rural Texas, correct?

DIXON: Well, my parents lived in the Houston suburbs, a little place called Humble. [winks] The Apollo missions were obviously a part of local history around there. But I really grew up on my granddaddy's ranch. Couple thousand acres, all the cow pies you could eat. [winks again]

METAXA: Something in your eye, Lieutenant?

MAGNUS: So, wide open plains, fresh air—

DIXON: You got it.

METAXA: Then what makes you think you'll be able to function in a confined environment? Big fella like you especially.

DIXON: Naw, if it gets stuffy, I'll just crack open a window.

TIMESTAMP—11:52 AM

DIXON: Anyone else feelin' peckish?

METAXA: [makes note on paper]

MAGNUS: [takes sip of water]

DIXON: Do shrinks get hungry, or do ya guys just feed off the energy of your subjects?

METAXA: Let's just cut the B.S. and get straight to the reason you're here. Why should we let you up there?

DIXON: [rolls pencil between fingers] I grew up a stone's throw from Mission Control. I watched every launch online. I was obsessed with the magic of the thing, still am. The way they'd arc through the sky, burst through the clouds... [demonstrates with pencil] As a boy, I vowed to get there. And I've almost made it. [places pencil behind ear] I work hard. I give my best each day. [rises from chair, turns to exit then turns back] I may act carefree, but I sure as hell ain't careless.

Subject is opinionated, brash, arrogant. A loner with charisma. Blunt, very blunt. But his work ethic is unimpeachable. He's passionate. Driven.

An egotist? Absolutely. An astronaut? As far as I am concerned, they are one and the same.

—Dr. Stephen Metaxa

When Abrams, Topfsky, and Florez returned, they were masked, gloved, and goggled. Duvvur's corpse remained a watchful observer, bobbing above as they entered. Abrams found most difficult tasks in his life easier if he broke them into smaller pieces. It appeared the bullet had done that part. Bits of brain clung to the bulkhead like barnacles. Flesh and gore drifted overhead.

Abrams gagged. The odor had grown so overpowering that he pressed an absorbent cloth against the mask. It had little effect.

Naidoo, carefully examining the body, turned to address them. "The cause of death is clear," she said. "Let's treat the commander's body with respect, clean this up the best we can."

For a few seconds, Florez didn't move, he just stared wide-eyed at the gore. Topfsky blocked her nose with the crook of her arm. "Aghh... Why the hell use a gun? Put us all in danger."

Abrams shook his head. "No, it was thought out. No windows in the botany lab. And the reinforced aluminum could sustain a gun blast."

The trio silently began their work. Abrams moved forward and examined the basil plants morosely—scarlet droplets dotted the leaves like morning dew. He mused on the horrific absurdity of a dead body 230 miles above a nuclear holocaust. Topfsky alternately sighed audibly and gagged. Florez still hadn't said a word.

"God, this is unbelievable," muttered Topfsky. She swiped a skull fragment out of the air.

Gradually, they grew desensitized. As they neared completion, Abrams's gloves were dyed dark red. He looked at them and shivered. Naidoo did what she could to restore their commander's nobility, scrubbing his face and wrapping his head in thick gauze to conceal the true extent of the wound.

Florez had been sent to retrieve additional materials. The astronaut returned with an armful of towelettes, his mask off and trailing behind him by a single strap. "We don't have too many more of these. I checked the—"

"Florez, watch where you're—" Topfsky's warning came too late, as Florez floated headfirst into a bloody fog. He clawed at his face and rubbed at his eyes, weak sputters evolving into hacking coughs. Florez wailed, releasing the towelettes and bumping into a wall as he fled the lab. Abrams started after him. Naidoo blocked his way.

"Give him a bit," she said. "Time alone will do him good."

"The man needs to talk to someone!"

"The man needs to wash up, pull himself together, and finish this job," declared Naidoo. Sweat glistened on her ebony skin.

"You're acting like a science experiment went wrong," Topfsky cried. "Duvvur is dead!"

"Or murdered." Dixon would have sauntered in if there had been gravity. He still managed a kind of weightless swagger.

Red, Sadakov, and Sho arrived more tentatively behind him. Six astronauts watched as their new commander approached their old commander and gently closed the corpse's eyes. Only then did Abrams feel like he could breathe again.

¤

"Jump to no conclusions!" Naidoo pointed a bloodstained finger at the Texan.

Dixon put a hand to her shoulder. "Course not, Doo, but don't dismiss it either. Give this a think, now." The astronaut raised three fingers of his own. "Three guns. That's how many we got up here—one for each of our Russki pals." Topfsky's eyes narrowed. "If the commander wanted to kill himself—boom, splat, and the gun wouldn't be his problem anymore..." Dixon bit down on his lip, considering his next words carefully. "If it was a murder weapon, though, maybe the killer woulda returned it where he or she..." He glanced at Topfsky. "... got it from. Ya know, so as not to arouse ..." His eyes met Sadakov's. "... suspicion."

"The guns issued to us are tools, nothing more, among many in our survival kits," Red started.

"But why?" asked Abrams. "Why have firearms in a space station?"

"Voskhod 2."

"I'm sorry?"

Red repeated himself. "Voskhod 2. Man's first spacewalk in nineteen sixty-five. Alexey Leonav and Pavel Belyayev manned the craft. They landed safely, but there was a timing error. They were stranded, alone, under the trees of the Russian taiga. The cosmonauts spent a frigid night huddled together in their capsule, the howls of wolves echoing into the night. They were rescued, but the dangers of the wilderness proved pistols a necessity."

Dixon inspected his fingernails. "The commander wasn't a wolf, but that don't make him any less dead."

Sadakov ground his teeth. "I will not stand for these baseless accusations."

The Texan raised his arms in mock surrender. "Nobody is accusing nobody."

"But what you are suggesting is very serious." Naidoo's voice was firm.

"Oh, I know it," said Dixon. "I'm not takin' any of this lightly."

Sadakov exhaled, air hissing between his teeth. "Dixon could make light of a black hole."

Dixon ignored the jab. "Well there's no harm in checkin' 'em out, is there? We could have a killer on board, folks. I can't be the only one feelin' the slightest sense of urgency."

The crew members began looking to Naidoo. She straightened. "We will search the survival kits."

Red's forehead creased. "Those kits are property of the Russian gov—"

"I suspect there is no Russian government. Not any longer." Sho lingered behind the crowd. "No politicians, no nations, no allegiances. Only us." Red looked away.

"I suppose there is no harm in a simple inspection," Topfsky said, her eyes closed like the corpse in the room's far corner. "One of our guns *was* used, after all."

"It would be a violation of trust. A breach of privacy," Sadakov growled.

Naidoo pursed her lips. "I've made my decision. Is that understood?" Five of the six astronauts nodded, some mumbling in agreement. "Sadakov, is that understood?"

The Russian fumed. "Yes, Commander."

¤

Dixon led the procession, Naidoo followed close behind. Stoic and silent, the seven astronauts flowed into the cargo hold.

Naidoo gave a quick scan. "The guns. Where are they kept?"

Topfsky pointed to a collection of three storage lockers. "There should be one in each."

Dixon unlatched the first locker—Sadakov's. After rummaging through its contents for a few moments, he pulled out a survival kit and opened it. The glint of a 9mm Makarov pistol was immediate and striking.

Dixon deftly removed the magazine cartridge. "No missing bullets." But another object stole his attention. Dixon whistled, slowly unsheathing a machete, admiring the blade as he attempted a few experimental slashes through the air. "You folks got some real Robinson Crusoe shit…"

"Put that down," Sadakov hissed.

The Texan did so reluctantly. He cocked his head. "For wolves, too, I suppose?"

"It's for heavy foliage," explained Red.

"And cutting egos down to size," Topfsky added. Dixon was already unlatching the second box—Topfsky's.

Abrams squinted. "Is it there?" The Texan dug around a bit, then nodded. This one was fully loaded as well. As Dixon approached the final locker, the tension in the room congealed like the blood in the botany lab.

Dixon's pace slowed. He retrieved the survival kit and unlatched it with a flourish. As he peered inside, a tinge of uncertainty replaced his boldness. He knit his brow.

"Well?" asked Naidoo.

Dixon slowly shook his head. The corners of his mouth arched. In a moment, his hubris was reignited. He turned to the third Russian. "Red-handed."

Red rushed to see for himself. "I don't understand…" His voice trembled. "Someone must have taken the gun from my locker. I don't know where it is."

Dixon crossed his arms. "The killer does."

Red was breathing heavily; he made a turn to exit. "I should find Florez."

Abrams nodded. "I'll join you."

Naidoo was quick to block their path. "Hold on. We have to—"

"What? Just keep everyone here until one of us confesses, is that it?" asked Topfsky.

Naidoo was careful to steady her voice. "There's a gun missing from the botany lab, a gun missing from the storage locker. One of you..."

"Whose to say it ain't you, Doo?" Dixon pointed and stabbed the air. "Duvvur died and left you Queen."

"You're full of kak. I'm trained as a medic! I don't—"

"You don't want to stay either," Topfsky interrupted. "You voted to leave."

Dixon nodded. "Mighty convenient for ya, seeing that the leave camp's gained some ground."

"Back off! Both of you." Sadakov's nostrils flared.

The Texan whistled. "Well, well, well. How quickly Dimitri turns his coat. Fancy yourself Deputy Sheriff, Mr. Sadakov?"

"Shut up, David." Like a serpent, a violet vein wound up the side of the Russian's forehead, disappearing under his shaggy black mane.

"Come to think of it, you didn't wanna stick aroun' here either, did ya, Dimitri? I mean, who's to say they didn't collaborate?"

Sadakov lunged at Dixon, gripped the collar of the Texan's shirt, and yanked him forward. Dixon met the Russian's outrage with a goofy grin. Sadakov sneered. "You lie through those teeth."

The smiling astronaut picked at a molar with his tongue. "Got the balls to knock 'em out?"

The two remained nose to nose. The cargo hold was soundless. For a moment, the Russian considered the query, curling his fingers. But instead of throwing a punch, he sprayed Dixon's face with saliva and pushed him aside. Sadakov made for the door; the crew parted before him. Even Naidoo backed down at his fury. Dixon's laughter followed him down the corridor.

¤

PSYCHOLOGICAL EVALUATION

Expedition 145
Subject: Dimitri Sadakov
Born: 8/1/95; Omsk, Russia

Subject was cooperative, though his responses seem to be carefully calculated. This behavior appears less a sign of deception and more likely an intense determination. Subject knows what he wants, and his answers, though largely preconceived, proved him worthy.

Included are excerpts of key exchanges.

METAXA: Welcome. Go ahead and grab a chair, Mr. Sadakov.

SADAKOV: Thank you. [takes seat]

MAGNUS: You already know that you're one of the top candidates for the crew...

SADAKOV: Yes, sir. And allow me again to express my gratitude—

METAXA: Careful now, you haven't been selected just yet.

SADAKOV: Of... course.

MAGNUS: Still have to decide if you're fit for space travel.

METAXA: We should probably address the most prominent negative on your transcript first. [holds up a document, pointing toward a highlighted paragraph]

SADAKOV: Are you referring to the Korolev incident?

METAXA: [nods] Your Roscosmos superiors recorded two emotional outbursts and five peer complaints. Can you explain that?

SADAKOV: I was a young engineer. I had yet to learn temperance. Others on the staff were mishandling sensitive equipment and dangerous chemicals. I snapped at the incompetence. I should have... kept a more level head.

MAGNUS: You threw a test tube.

SADAKOV: An empty one.

METAXA: As it was nearly a decade ago... Did you change this behavior? Did you seek help?

SADAKOV: Anger management. I'm proud to say nothing like
the poor choices I made in Korolev have occurred since
that unfortunate day.

TIMESTAMP—3:29 PM

MAGNUS: Why an astronaut?

SADAKOV: I think we have come to a point where we as a
world need to begin to look outward. Mankind is united
like never before. There was a time not long ago when an
American and a Russian journeying together in a capsule
was unthinkable. If anything, we have to continually
embrace the significance of that, lest we return to the way
it was before.

MAGNUS: I see.

SADAKOV: I'm connected to that historical narrative, by my
heritage. My father's grandfather had a part to play.

METAXA: In what?

SADAKOV: Sputnik.

MAGNUS: Your great-grandfather, an engineer?

SADAKOV: The project's propagandist. One of them, anyway.
He looked at things like I do, I think. He saw the dual
nature of every technological advancement—the scientific
and the... symbolic.

METAXA: Interesting. Do you conflate science with art,
expressive forms?

SADAKOV: [shakes head] You misunderstand. A wise man once said, "Art is more godlike than science. Science discovers; art creates." They are not the same. But we can seek meaning from science.

MAGNUS: It's like the old proverb. "In scientia veritas, in arte honestas." [pauses] I minored in Latin.

METAXA: [rolls his eyes] What's it mean?

MAGNUS: In science truth...

SADAKOV: [nods] ...in art honor.

TIMESTAMP—4:07 PM

METAXA: So, are you looking to follow in your great-grandfather's legacy by having an active role in space faring?

SADAKOV: No.

METAXA: Care to elaborate?

SADAKOV: He dedicated his life to using science to promote rivalry, antagonism. I want to use mine to ensure cooperation.

Subject has clear priorities and noble goals. It seems that his anger has ebbed, replaced with a gritty determination.

— Prof. Edward Magnus

¤

Abrams found Florez attached to the station's treadmill by hook and harness, but the machine wasn't moving. The astronaut was just standing there, staring straight ahead. Abrams watched Florez double over to cough, a bit of phlegm flying from his mouth and breaking apart as it floated away. His cheeks flushed a deep red when he realized he was not alone.

"Not feeling too hot?" Abrams asked.

Florez nodded glumly.

"Mind some company?"

The astronaut shrugged. For a moment, Abrams allowed the man to gather himself before he spoke again. "This was Duvvur's favorite spot."

"The commander did love his exercise." The corners of Florez's lips raised in a half-smile. "The irony of a 'beefy Hindu'... Dixon thought that was hilarious." He snorted. "Maybe the pull of the harness reminded him of home. The feeling of gravity, the ground under your feet."

"Could be." They stared into nothing. Like a sliver of sunlight breaking through a thick canopy, metal glimmered for a moment in Florez's palm before once again being obscured by a closed fist. The concern on Abrams's face must have shown, so Florez hesitantly uncurled his fingers. A brass bullet. Speckled red.

"Such a small thing. I found it lodged next to a console in the lab when I returned to look for a..." The astronaut absent-mindedly rubbed his still-grimy cheek. "I couldn't find a towel." He sighed. "Damn it all, Abes. This expedition was supposed to be my second chance."

"How so?"

"You know this isn't my first time up here."

"Sure, you and Red both. Sho too."

Florez drew a felt patch out of his pocket; loose threads dangled beneath it like jellyfish tentacles. Expedition 132. "Commander Avery liked to call it Expedition 666... It was a routine repair, but..." Florez rubbed the insignia between his fingers. "No one forgets their first spacewalk. The two of us out there. Red claims I kept saying 'wow, wow, wow.' Like a hundred times. I don't remember any of that." He shook his head. "I wasn't looking at the incomprehensible beauty of our planet or the vastness of the universe. No, instead I was fixated on the tether. That tug at my back. All I could think about was how close I was—to complete and total freedom." In seeing Abrams's reaction, Florez backtracked. "Not that I wanted that, mind you. It's just... when you stand at a cliff's edge, sometimes all you think about is the fall, you know?"

Abrams nodded hesitantly.

"And then I froze up. And before I knew it, my toolkit wasn't in my hands anymore. It went spiraling away, scratching along the solar panels like I was keying a hundred-billion-dollar car. Total screw-up. A maintenance mission became a potential emergency."

"And yet they let you back up."

"They never found out. Thanks to Duvvur. He was the First Officer on Expedition 131, you see. Told NASA it was a malfunction instead of an accident."

Abrams frowned. "Lying like that'll get an astronaut grounded for life."

"You don't have to tell me. He risked his career to save my sorry ass." Florez spun the bullet in the air in front of him like a hovering top. "And when the time came, I wasn't there to save his."

"Like you could have anticipated what would happen..."

Florez looked him in the eye. "What the hell did happen?"

Abrams didn't have an answer.

"Maybe it doesn't matter." Florez brushed back his hair. Abrams's eyes narrowed. He noticed strands were graying.

"You should have Naidoo take a look at you."

Florez snagged the bullet out of the air. "She has enough on her plate."

"Whatever the case, I'm not sure you've had enough on yours. You've barely been eating, Gabriel." The astronaut had been lean before the launch, but now he was downright skeletal.

"I'm fine." Florez prepared to pull away, but Abrams held him down.

"You can choose not to accept help, that's your prerogative. You can even continue your 'screw-it-all' diet, if you want. But you're not fine, Florez. None of us are fine. Duvvur is dead, tensions are high, and we're stuck orbiting a world that's blowing itself back to the Dark Ages!"

Florez put his head in his hands. He began to speak, but every few words were staccatoed by a sob. "Emma... my wife... she promised... she promised she'd whip up something special... for when... for when..." Florez lifted his head. Tears bubbled down his cheeks, wiping clean the caked coffee powder and dried crimson that dusted his face.

Abrams's face softened; he wrapped an arm around him. Florez sheepishly opened his palm to hand him the bullet. It hovered there between them. Abrams snatched it and clutched it to his chest.

¤

The commander looked more dignified in his spacesuit, to be sure. His fishbowl helmet dimmed his lifeless features. Heavy pads gave his limp limbs the illusion of strength. The corpse appeared almost peaceful in the airlock, and Abrams hoped that tranquility would accompany the rest of the commander's journey. Duvvur might circle the globe, an eternal satellite. No rest, just an endless dance with Earth's gravity.

But Abrams feared a more tumultuous final flight. A terrible coincidence of angle and velocity might set Duvvur on a collision course with Earth's atmosphere. Like a falling meteor, the commander would plummet in a ball of searing flame.

Red and Sho stepped away from the airlock, having already taken their moments alone to say goodbye. Topfsky, Dixon, and Naidoo were already there, floating in respectful silence. Sadakov hovered apart, brooding in the darkness of the module's far side. Abrams remained and approached the body, bending over it for a moment before giving Duvvur a final farewell pat on the shoulder.

An astronaut's cremation. Abrams stole a glance toward the fiery planet below. *At least one of us may find his way home.*

Florez's wheezy breaths immediately signaled his presence. He looked terrible. For some reason, the first image that came to Abrams's mind when he saw the man was that of an old whaling vessel at sea. Florez's eyes were foggy. Abrams imagined his bones creaking like rotting boards, his body teetering like a hull set upon by heavy surf.

"The commander believed in reincarnation," Abrams consoled him. "Surely that counts for something."

The mist in Florez's eyes crystalized into bitter ice. "Yeah, well, not much good that'd do, unless we all come back as cockroaches."

"Talk about a nuclear family," Dixon muttered.

Sho pursed his lips. "Do not discredit this notion. The Hindu faith emphasizes a cycle of destruction and creation.

Perhaps this idea provided the commander solace in his final days."

"It did." Red cleared his throat. "Each night, since the first bomb was dropped, I noticed Duvvur reading from his sacred texts. I watched him, meditating over the words. Looking for answers." The Russian hesitated. "I... After what happened, I found this." Red revealed a little volume, its pages yellowed and dog-eared.

"Most of his books were in Sanskrit," the astronaut explained, thumbing through the pages. "Luckily, this one has an English translation." The corner of one page had been folded in, and Red reverently smoothed it out. "He marked this passage. May I?" The Russian looked to Naidoo.

"You and Florez knew Duvvur the longest."

Florez nodded solemnly.

In an odd juxtaposition of the archaic and the futuristic, Red held the book up to the space station's fluorescent lights:

> Burn him not up, nor quite consume him, Agni: let not his
> body or his skin be scattered,
> O all possessing Fire, when thou hast matured him, then
> send him on his way unto the Fathers.
> When thou hast made him ready, all possessing Fire, then
> do thou give him over to the Fathers,
> When he attains unto the life that waits him, he shall
> become subject to the will of gods.

The Sun receive thine eye, the Wind thy breath; go, as thy merit is, to earth or heaven.

Red closed the volume and handed it to Florez, who received it with trembling fingers. Abrams watched carefully as Florez placed it deftly in the crook of Duvvur's arm. Then, one by one, each astronaut left their commander behind. As Abrams headed for the crew quarters, he heard the airlock door shut. He didn't turn around.

¤

PSYCHOLOGICAL EVALUATION

Expedition 144
Subject: Clifford Kaznach
Born: 5/22/92; District of Columbia, United States

Subject's story is Hollywood-worthy. The product of a scandalous affair between American and Russian diplomats during intense negotiations, his birth cost his mother her job and his father his reputation. Straddling two citizenships and overcoming the perceived disgrace of his origins, he earned two advanced degrees in aeronautics and climbed the ladder in Roscosmos. His tale is truly remarkable.

Included are excerpts of key exchanges.

<u>TIMESTAMP—11:35 AM</u>

METAXA: Take a seat, please.

MAGNUS: Surely you're exhausted, so we'll try not to keep
you too long.

KAZNACH: [sits] Oh, I'm used to the travel, but thank you all
the same. Whenever either of my parents left for business
across the sea, they said they were "heading out to stretch
their legs." I like to think I've inherited that attitude.

METAXA: Your English is impeccable.

KAZNACH: So is yours. [laughs] Of course, my father was an
American. But you already know that.

MAGNUS: [smiles] Could be.

METAXA: I think he's caught on to our charade, Eddie.
[chuckles]

MAGNUS: We're taking a diplomatic approach. I'm sure you
can tell us all about that.

KAZNACH: [plays with his wedding ring] Foreign affairs.
[glances up at the two psychologists] What? You think I
haven't heard all the jokes? In the media, I was portrayed
as a mistake. An international slip-up. It isn't true, you
know. I've always argued that I'm the reason the talks
were a success.

MAGNUS: How so?

KAZNACH: I was what kept the Americans willing to negotiate for so long. Nothing like knowing your baby's in the belly of the woman at the other side of the table to keep someone an interested party.

MAGNUS: Ah.

KAZNACH: My life has been defined by compromise.

TIMESTAMP—12:08 PM

METAXA: Tell me about Expedition 132.

KAZNACH: There's not much more to tell than what you've read, I'm sure.

MAGNUS: You were present at the failed EVA.

METAXA: You and Officer Florez both.

KAZNACH: [shifts in seat] It was... routine maintenance. Took a nasty turn.

METAXA: Commander Avery seemed to suspect the solar panel malfunction was triggered through human error.

KAZNACH: I suppose the timing might point to something like that. EVA one day, faulty solar panel the next. But everything looked to be in perfect shape, at least when we were out there. [leans back in his chair] First Officer Duvvur suggested it may have been caused by space debris. Seems a valid theory.

KAZNACH: I couldn't avoid politics no matter how hard I tried.
Believe me, I despised what I had born into. [pauses]
Space was my escape. The pursuit of science has no
borders, or at least it shouldn't be political. No double
dealing. Everyone shares a common goal.

METAXA: And what's that? In your mind.

KAZNACH: A shift in perspective. No one seems to be able to see
things outside of their own little world. Discovery allows
humanity to... well, to look up. It creates a united front,
you know? When Neil took his small step, for a moment it
wasn't 'us against them.' It was 'us versus the universe.'

Subject clearly has fought an uphill battle to reach his
current status, and his experience and expertise will be an
ideal addition to the crew. I was particularly struck by the
quote I've elected to place at the end of this evaluation.

— Prof. Edward Magnus

KAZNACH: On Expedition 132... I saw the entire planet. All of
it, just in front of me. And, get this, all those lines you see
on the maps? They aren't there.

PART TWO

Overboard

"It is a great misfortune to be alone, my friends; and it must be believed that solitude can quickly destroy reason."

—Jules Verne,
The Mysterious Island

PSYCHOLOGICAL EVALUATION

Expedition 146
Eva Topfsky
Born: 12/7/94; Volgodonsk, Russia

Subject presents a curious case. She was raised in a creative environment, but has chosen to suppress this mindset in favor of rationality and logic. Indeed, evidence of this constant struggle can be identified throughout the testing period.

Included are excerpts of key exchanges.

TIMESTAMP—2:00 PM

TOPFSKY: Hello, am I in the right place?

MAGNUS: [rises] You must be Ms. Topfsky.

TOPFSKY: And I suppose that makes you Doctor Metaxa...

MAGNUS: Magnus, actually. Professor Edward Magnus. [offers outstretched hand]

TOPFSKY: [places thick folder in his hand] Those are my medical evaluations, performance history, a copy of my birth certificate, a list of scenarios in which my skill set might come into use—

METAXA: Ms. Topfsky, we've already read a great deal about you. Contrary to what you may believe, we're concerned about the contents of your mind rather than that of your résumé.

MAGNUS: [drops folder on table] Meet my associate, Doctor
    Stephen Metaxa.

TOPFSKY: Charmed. [sits]

METAXA: Why don't we start with a few simple psychological
    tests.

TOPFSKY: Very well.

MAGNUS: [raises ink blot test] Mind telling me what you see?

TOPFSKY: Certainly. I see a Rorschach test, invented in 1921
    by Hermann Rorschach, used to examine a subject's
    personality and mental state.

MAGNUS: You're taking this a bit literally...

TOPFSKY: Is there any other way to take things? I could
    have pretended. Called it a butterfly. Or a face. But that
    wouldn't be telling the truth, would it?

MAGNUS: I suppose not.

METAXA: [grabs a marker and notepad and writes with quick
    strokes, turns it around: Candor A+] Satisfied?

TOPFSKY: Not particularly.

MAGNUS: Let's move along, shall we?

TIMESTAMP—2:40 PM

TOPFSKY: [eyes cup of water]

MAGNUS: What's the matter, want something stronger?

TOPFSKY: I don't drink.

METAXA: Why's that, Ms. Topfsky?

TOPFSKY: My father.

MAGNUS: An alcoholic.

TOPFSKY: A concert pianist. A good one, too. He would be
gone for long stretches, either abroad playing in music
halls or in the study in our apartment, hunched over the
old grand piano. When I was very young he used to let
me sit on his lap as he played. I used to try to catch his
hands. I never could. His hands were like lightning—there
one moment, gone another. Then mother died, and my
father began locking the study. Sometimes I would still
try to listen to the music through the oak door. But it was
muffled, distorted. I couldn't tell if it was Rachmaninoff or
Rubinstein. Then one day... [sips water]

MAGNUS: Please, continue.

TOPFSKY: Then one day, the music stopped. And the door did
not open. The militsiya found their way in, but that was
days later, and only after the landlord heard my weeping.
My memory is... There are blank spaces from that time.
I did not leave the side of that door until they forcibly
removed me.

METAXA: Your father—

TOPFSKY: He died where he lived—slumped over his prized
piano, surrounded by empty liquor bottles.

MAGNUS: Alcohol poisoning.

TOPFSKY: [shakes head] The alcohol did the deed, yes. But
his true killer was a poisoned mind. Detached. Obsessed.
Slowly corrupted until it was undone.

METAXA: Ms. Topfsky, do you believe your father was a good
    man?

TOPFSKY: No worse than any other man. Though that is not
    saying much.

Subject is Type A, no question. The true query lies in
whether or not this would be an asset or a disadvantage
aboard the station. Her tightly-wound and meticulous nature
could certainly provide a much-needed counterpoint to the
more cocksure astronaut tendencies. She's a hard woman,
practical, with a sobering outlook.

                                      — Dr. Stephen Metaxa

¤

"Are you... drunk?"

Abrams pushed himself beside Topfsky, who was curled
at the right turn of a corridor. The engineer didn't respond.
She forced a liquid bubble out of a silver canister, stared at it
blankly for a moment, and then swallowed it whole. The silence
was broken only by a Russian belch a few moments later. Then
Abrams cleared his throat.

"Dixon was right, you Russians are vodka-guzzlers." Topfsky
actually giggled, and Abrams mused that the laugh seemed
about as out of place as the Ruskova in her hands. "Never
thought you'd qualify."

"I'm a... floating stereotype, aren't I?" Her face soured. "God, this stuff's awful. I don't know why Red raves about it."

"I thought you didn't..."

She belched again. "I don't." She wrinkled her nose.

More silence. Topfsky made her way to a window and peered out at their graying planet. Two weeks after the bombings ended, and still fires raged, now partially obscured under a heavy blanket of airborne soot.

"Noah, why did this happen?"

"I don't know. Fear? Fate? Hubris?"

"I don't mean down there."

"Up here?" He sighed. "Same answer."

"It's like a cruel joke." Abrams searched for words, stopping short after meeting Topfsky's eyes and finding them wet with tears. "I'm scared, Noah."

"We're all scared. We couldn't possibly have been prepared for—"

"Not *that*." Her breathing was ragged.

Abrams's eyes narrowed. "What are you talking about?"

"Space." She inhaled another globule of vodka, as if the word itself was a sufficient explanation. After a pause, Topfsky continued. "It's... Something feels wrong up here."

"Eva, you voted to stay. You were more confident than anyone..." He scratched at the stubble on his chin. "I don't—"

"Take the war. If we were down there, assuming we managed to find safety before the initial blasts, each nuke would shake us to our core. Fires might consume us if nuclear winter didn't freeze us first. Ash would blot out the sky. It must be hell down there." She rubbed the canister between her hands. "But from where we are, our dying world is a light show." She grit her teeth. "A beautiful light show. And, wouldn't you know it, we've got front row seats." Topfsky turned the canister on its head, shaking it up and down. A few meager droplets sprinkled out, the stray bubbles wandering about the cabin.

"Even Duvvur..." she whispered. Abrams waited for her to finish her sentence, but she just watched the droplets tumble and collide.

"You're not saying..."

"It was horrible. But don't pretend you didn't see the beauty in it." Topfsky wiggled her fingers through the air. "The way the fluorescent lights made the blood shimmer."

Abrams shook his head. "You're not well." He pushed himself upward. "I'm finding Naidoo."

"No. Please don't burden her further."

He glanced down the corridor.

"Up here, it's all wrong," she said again. "Space has this way of making the bad things..." She poked at a bubble of vodka. "...the destructive, the catastrophic... somehow entrancing." Topfsky took a deep breath. The back of Abrams's neck was slick with sweat. He just stared at her.

She continued, "I chose to pursue numbers because numbers make sense. They are concrete. Logical. Even chaos can be explained away." She twirled a limp lock of dark hair, pulling it behind her ear. "In space, there is no direction. In a very literal sense, and in one... less so." A pause. "Has it not crossed your mind that space is changing us? The crew?"

For a second, Abrams's lips moved but no sound escaped. "Eva." Her eyes met his once again. He felt like she was begging for a question, so he complied. "You didn't—"

"No, I would never. He was a good man, a strong leader. But what happened did not surprise me. *That* is why I'm frightened."

"I... I should probably be getting to Naidoo." He began a slow exit, using his hands to propel himself away.

"Noah..." He turned. "Up here, Earth's laws need not apply."

"You already said. Gravity doesn't tether us down."

"No." Topfsky's mouth was rigid. "*All* of Earth's laws."

Abrams paled.

¤

"Abrams... Abrams... Noah!"

The astronaut drew in air sharply. The blurry figure floating before him came into focus. "Jesus Christ, Red, I'm awake! What're you—"

The Russian put a finger to his lips. "It's Florez," he hissed. "He—there's something very wrong."

Abrams groggily unfastened the straps that held him in place. He rubbed the bridge of his nose. "Where?"

"The aft."

Abrams and Red cruised soundlessly, taking care to avoid other sleeping crew members. They came across Sho, bobbing unrestrained. The man occasionally elected to sleep without strapping himself in. Sho insisted that it reminded him of his childhood at sea. Abrams thought it was absurd. There were nine sleeping pads for the nine astronauts. Abrams winced. *Eight*.

One earbud curled from Sho's ear. The sound of waves breaking helped the astronaut sleep. Abrams gestured toward the man, who was snoring softly as he drifted about the cabin.

"Don't wake him," Red whispered. "No one can know."

Abrams grimaced. "Why so secretive?"

"It's necessary. For Florez's safety."

"If it's a health issue, you should have Naidoo look him over."

"Not her. She'd feel obligated to tell the crew."

"And what's the harm in that?"

"It's too dangerous. The crew's barely keeping it together as it is. For now, this is just between you and me."

They paused. The snoring had ceased. "And me."

Their heads swiveled. Sho's eyes were open, and he was glaring. "Lead the way." Abrams looked to Red. Red shrugged.

They plugged their noses as they approached the aft. A cocktail of vomit, sputum, and blood wafted down the corridor. Someone was retching. Red halted just before the entranceway. "Florez is... ill," he managed. "Take these." He pulled a collection of surgical masks from a pocket, and offered one each to Abrams and Sho. Sho's eyebrow arched, but the two astronauts did as they were told and inched forward.

Abrams gagged. Hunched in a corner, Florez was surrounded by a flurry of coughed-up fluid and trembling like a dog left in the rain. He seemed to have aged dramatically since Abrams last saw him—his skin sallow and sagging. Whole tangled clumps of hair had fallen free around the astronaut, spiraling like tumbleweed. "N-no... You weren't supposed to tell anyone but... anyone but..." A hacking cough left him panting. "Anyone but Abrams."

"I know," said Red. "But Sho doesn't miss much."

Abrams braced himself against a bulkhead. "What the hell's going on?"

"Can't you see?" Florez sputtered. "I'm infected. Diseased." The next cough was bloodier. "If she... finds out. She'll kill me. And they'll let her."

"Who would kill you?" asked Sho.

"Naidoo. Just like she killed Duvvur."

"You think..." A thousand thoughts bombarded Abrams at once. "What makes you so sure?"

"We've worked it all out," Red began. "Duvvur was infected with some kind of contagion. He must have come to Naidoo for medical assistance, and Naidoo killed him to prevent the spread of the disease."

Sho frowned. "What evidence could you possibly have that the commander was afflicted?"

Florez licked yellowing teeth. "Cause I was exposed. In the lab. The symptoms followed almost immediately," he rasped.

"Topfsky, Naidoo, and I were there too," reminded Abrams.

"Yes," Florez agreed. "Masked and gloved." He wheezed. "My face was open to the elements."

Sho and Abrams made eye contact. After a long pause, Abrams asked, "What... are we supposed to do now?"

"It seems to me these men are plotting mutiny." Sho spoke with his signature calm.

"Oh, don't be so dramatic," muttered Florez.

Red shook his head. "We're not scheming in the dark—"

"That's exactly what you're doing," countered Abrams.

"Look around." Red glanced down the corridor. "Topfsky's headed for a breakdown, Dixon and Sadakov are too embroiled in their own egos to look at the big picture, and Naidoo's so-called pragmatism keeps us alive at the expense of our humanity."

Abrams exhaled. "Naidoo is the acting commander."

"And she's a good actress, I'll give her that," Florez wheezed.

There was a prolonged silence. "Noah, Yamato. Stand with us." Red reached out a hand; neither took it.

Sho cleared his throat. "We are broken men and women. The stresses of our... situation have created fractures both within us and between us. The solution is not to embrace these divisions, but to heal them. You cannot be blamed for your re-actionary behavior. I do understand why you jumped to those... conclusions." The man looked to Abrams. "For that reason, we will not reveal your treachery if you do not force our hands." He turned around.

"Where are you going?" barked Florez.

"We are bringing your malady to the attention of the crew." He started down the corridor. "Come along, Noah."

¤

PSYCHOLOGICAL EVALUATION

Expedition 146
Subject: Yamato Sho
Born: 3/26/89; Hamanaka, Japan

Subject is a man of few words, but his knowledge seems boundless. His pursuit of lofty goals from humble beginnings is inspiring, and his pioneering work in astrophysics has been groundbreaking.

It is clear that Subject's upbringing largely influences his character. Deeply-ingrained lessons in respect and humility shine through in his demeanor.

Included are excerpts of key exchanges.

TIMESTAMP—9:15 AM

MAGNUS: Good morning, Doctor Sho, pleasure to meet you. Thank you for taking time out of your day to come and speak with us. I'm Edward Magnus.

SHO: I know. The pleasure is all mine, professor. I am familiar with your work.

METAXA: [coughs]

SHO: And yours, Doctor Metaxa.

MAGNUS: Well let's get right to it, shall we?

SHO: Certainly.

METAXA: Now this wouldn't be your first expedition...

SHO: No, sir. My third voyage. [bows his head] Not bad for a poor fisherman's son.

METAXA: Yes. Tell us more about your childhood, would you?

SHO: I grew up in a small fishing community. [chuckles softly] My father was a bit of a local legend there. He had a reputation for hauling in massive catches. [takes a breath] Nishin was his specialty. I believe you call them kippers.

MAGNUS: [turns to Metaxa] Red herring. Delicious.

SHO: Much of my early life was spent out on the sea. Nothing but blue—often for days at a time. [traces table's NASA insignia with his finger] I would say those experiences, more than anything else really, were what prepared me for the isolation of space.

MAGNUS: Your father—he was quite the influence then?

SHO: [nods] I have never known a more humble man. "Fishing is easy," he would tell me. "They form schools, blindly follow one another. Keep a step ahead, and the nets will fill themselves."

TIMESTAMP—9:44 AM

MAGNUS: You've spent a lot of time on the station, certainly more than most. Does the monotony of the experience begin to gnaw at you?

SHO: Not so. The experience is magical—all of it.

METAXA: Any experience, even the most magical, grows tiresome after weeks of repetition...

SHO: Nonsense, doctor. Each day is a new day, a new adventure. And, fortunately, up there, a new day dawns every hour and half. [smiles mischievously]

TIMESTAMP—10:23 AM

METAXA: When you were a teen, you moved to... Shira... Shira...

SHO: Shiraishijima.

METAXA: Right. Near the city of Hiroshima, correct?

SHO: Not far.

METAXA: Surely the... horrors of the bomb had a profound impact on local culture.

SHO: [softly] My grandmother grew teary-eyed every August sixth.

METAXA: Do you believe these sentiments... had an effect on you?

SHO: Ah. You wonder if I harbor any resentment toward Americans. Perhaps your fears are warranted. But tell me this—do you gentlemen have lingering disdain for the German people? Do you spit where they walk and curse them for sinking the Lusitania? It is amazing what time can heal. Besides, citizens should not be held accountable for the actions of their state. People are not countries.

Subject is cerebral and insightful, a veteran of the space program and a seasoned astronaut. He is mentally sound in every capacity. Send him back up.

—Prof. Edward Magnus

¤

"Quarantine. It is the only reasonable solution," Naidoo concluded. The crew circled Florez like a group of surgeons, blue masks obscuring their faces so that only their eyes betrayed their fear.

Florez grunted. "And leave me unprotected so someone can finish me off like they did the commander." Florez erupted in a coughing attack. The crew shied away.

"Ok, let's say it *is* transferred by blood. How do we know it ain't transmitted by air?" Dixon's voice was muffled by his mask.

"What do you suppose we do then, Dixon, huh?" Red was crimson. "Suit him up, tie a rope to his leg, and drag him behind the station like a parade balloon?"

Dixon tilted his head as if he were actually considering the idea. "Six months, wasn't that the number ya gave us, Red? That leaves about twenty-two weeks until we start to starve." Dixon pointed to Florez. "I'm sorry, but he's dyin', bud. Every moment air circulates through his lungs is a risk to the crew. Every morsel he consumes is one less for the rest of us..."

Naidoo interrupted, "The cargo hold will do, and we'll supply you with antibiotics. And painkillers."

"Leaving me to rot," sputtered Florez. "That's what you're doing."

"Gabriel..." Her voice cracked. "I'm just giving the rest of us a fighting chance."

"What gives you the right to make these life and death decisions?" Red shouted. "You're the one who—"

"Red!" Abrams put a hand on his arm. "You know very well she was next to take authority after the departure of Expedition 144."

Naidoo glowered. "Like it or not, I am your commander."

Florez, head in hands, didn't look up. "*Duvvur* is my commander."

"Sadakov. Sho." She turned her head. "I trust you can show Mr. Florez the way to the hold?"

The two men floated forward, each grabbing an arm. "You bastards! She's a killer!" He struggled, and, for a moment, his rabid ferocity broke him free. Just as suddenly, he had Abrams by the collar. "Noah... Noah, talk sense to them. Naidoo's the one who's infected, not me. Dixon too. In the mind, see? Tell them, stop them—"

Florez was yanked backwards. For a moment, all was still. "N-noah?" Abrams could not meet his gaze. As Sadakov and Sho hauled him backwards, Florez bellowed, "Damn you! Damn you to hell! Just wait! I'll be dead in the morning, and it won't be the sickness! Just wait."

Five of them remained. "That'll be all for now," said Naidoo, as coolly as she could. "Remember to wear your masks for at least twelve hours." She eyed Dixon, then Red. "Let's try to get back to sleep." The commander launched herself down the corridor and around the corner.

Dixon shook his head. "The hold. I just moved my golf club there... Should off him while we have the chance."

"You're sick, you know that?" snarled Red.

"No, Florez is. I'm gonna keep us alive, pal."

Topfsky moved between them. "No one's going to touch Gabriel," she said, glaring at Dixon. She turned to Red. "But I do think this was the right move."

Red's face twisted. Then he slumped. "I don't want to live with the weight of a man's life on my shoulders."

"Just add it to the weight of the world," said Abrams. The four of them hovered there, wordless and worldless.

Dixon eyed the two Russians. "You know what they used to say…" He grinned malevolently. "Better dead than red."

Topfsky slapped him across the face, her nails slicing open his flesh, leaving bloody streaks across the top of his cheek. The Texan wiped his face, looked at the blood on his hands, then showed it to the others. His smile vanished.

"You people are scared, all of ya. 'Cuz you know I'm right." He was gone a moment later.

¤

Dinner the next evening was uncomfortable. Red was absent, presumably eating his ration on the other side of the station. So was Dixon. The rest of them chewed in silence. Tensions were high. So was the temperature. Abrams began to notice that his hair was slick with perspiration, as was Sadakov's brow. Beads of sweat were forming along Topfsky's neck. The air felt heavy, something they all seemed to realize at about the same time.

"Naidoo!" Dixon entered, flushed and reeling. "What the hell's going on?"

Topfsky fanned herself rapidly. "It's got to be 40 degrees!"

"Must be a malfunction in the coolant system..." said Sadakov slowly.

The commander nodded. "We need to figure out how serious this is. Topfsky, run a full-scale analysis on the computer. Take Dixon with you." Topfsky shot the Texan a look; he frowned and rubbed his still-raw cheek. "Sho and Sadakov, make sure all the EVA equipment is in order in case we have to make an emergency repair. Oh and Abrams, find Red. We need his experience in this area."

In the aft, all of Florez's possessions were gone, having been transported to the cargo hold. Every trace of the man was eradicated. There was now a haunting neatness to the area. *We're treating him like a ghost.* Abrams couldn't blame Red for not wanting to linger in this place. Suddenly, he knew where the astronaut would be.

The cargo hold was isolated from the rest of the station, a thick steel door separating the room like a prison cell. A pane of glass in the door's center provided a visual, and shouting loud enough allowed audible, though inefficient, conversation.

"Red," said Abrams. The Russian floated near the door.

"Abrams."

"Listen, we need—"

"Did I ever tell you how Jules Verne sent his three spacemen to the moon?"

"Not the time—"

"They were shot. Out of a huge gun."

There was a soft rapping on the glass, and a muffled voice behind the door.

"It's Abrams!" yelled Red.

More murmuring, now hostile.

"Florez doesn't want to talk."

"I'm not here for him."

"What, then?" He wiped his forehead. "And why is it so damn hot?"

"We're trying to figure that out. Clearly there's a problem with the coolant system..."

Red pulled himself up. "Could be the ammonia pump failing. Or maybe a leak. We need an analysis—"

"Topfsky's on it."

"And we need to prepare—"

"Sho and Sadakov have that covered." Abrams brushed his lip with the end of his thumb. "But Red, I think you need to brace for the possibility of a spacewalk."

The Russian inhaled. "Without any guidance from Mission Control."

"Unless you want to be slow-roasted, we don't have many options. And you're the only one who has the experience..."

"I'm not the only one."

¤

"Florez is in no state for an EVA." Naidoo crossed her arms. "I won't allow it."

Red's gaze yielded nothing. "Best of luck to you."

"That's selfish. And suicidal," Naidoo countered. Red shrugged.

Sweat glistened on the tip of Sho's nose, which he wiped as he addressed Red. "Topfsky thinks the Passive Thermal Control System's capabilities were exceeded. I'm inclined to agree," he explained. "We're going to have to check out the radiator system—the panels, the ammonia tubes, all of it." The astronaut hesitated, turning to Naidoo. "It is a two-person job."

The muscles in Naidoo's face shifted as her jaw clenched. "There's no talking you out of this, is there?"

Red shook his head. "We're a team. Florez has the real experience anyway."

The commander faced Topfsky. "Do we have any theories regarding the origin of the malfunction?"

The Russian glanced up from her notebook. "Heat from the station's systems clearly isn't dissipating properly. The machinery undoubtedly has been pretty severely strained in the last month, having to accommodate unforeseen crew members. The PTCS simply could not maintain temperature alone. So why didn't the Active System take over?" Topfsky flipped through a few pages. "There are several possibilities. A problem with the flow of circulating ammonia. Instruments indicate a leak of some kind may be preventing heat-collection, although the instruments could just as well be malfunctioning."

"Or the radiators themselves may be at fault," added Sadakov. The man's voice was hoarse. "The panels may have failed to fully extend. Or they may be damaged."

Abrams frowned. "And the source of the damage?"

"I have a hunch." The whites of Dixon's teeth revealed themselves for a moment. He lazily fanned himself. "Since the end of the world, my guess is that satellites have been falling out of the sky like chunks of clay at a skeet shoot."

Naidoo turned to the Texan. "You think we were struck?" Dixon nodded. "If that's the case, we need to assess the damage. And quickly. It could be worse than we fear." She closed her eyes. "Red—"

"You get both of us or neither of us."

"Damn you." Naidoo rubbed her temples. "Be suited and prepared at the airlock in forty minutes for emergency repair." Red raised an eyebrow. Naidoo sighed. "Both of you."

Thirty-nine minutes later, Red arrived at the airlock, Florez at his side. The tension in the commander's jaw had not been released. "Don't bladdy screw this up." Naidoo often returned to her native slang during moments of particular stress. She was barely holding back, Abrams could tell. She and Florez both. Though the astronaut did his best to conceal it, his clamped lips betrayed the coughing fit he struggled to contain.

Florez stooped to collect the space helmet that hovered just below him. Abrams grabbed it first. "Gabriel..." he whispered.

"Are you sure you can do this?"

"I'm not dead yet."

Abrams held out the helmet. "But last time—"

Florez snatched it out of his hands, eyes darting to ensure no one else heard what was said. "Was last time." He scowled and pulled himself closer to Abrams's face. "I hope you're good at keeping secrets."

Red and Florez had their helmets in the crooks of their arms. The commander couldn't get herself to look Florez in the eye. "You have everything?" Red nodded. "You know what to look for?" He nodded once more. She rung her hands. "Alright then..." Red nodded a third and final time, and the two donned their fishbowl helmets.

With Topfsky at the control panel, the airlock's inner door slid open with a whoosh. The two men stepped inside and attached each other's tethers with ease. Florez then turned and gave Topfsky a thumbs up to indicate they were prepared for depressurization. She returned the gesture, and the door closed shut. Her fingers hovered over the switch that would open the outer door, exposing them to the vacuum. Naidoo grabbed her arm.

Topfsky's face twisted. "Commander?"

"Wait." Naidoo activated the comm system and spoke into the microphone. "Red. Florez." Both men turned to face the crew through the reinforced glass. "Come back safe."

The pair saluted, and the door to space opened behind them.

¤

PSYCHOLOGICAL EVALUATION

Expedition 144
Subject: Gabriel Florez
Born: 11/5/93; Flagstaff, Arizona

Subject has demonstrated the ability to conduct himself calmly during an emergency situation. Taking on a leadership role during the infamous "Disaster 132" Expedition, Subject successfully aided in the restoration of station functions on the brink of collapse. This experience, coupled with his level-headedness during a period of intense stress, makes him a particularly appealing candidate for relaunch.

Included are excerpts of key exchanges.

TIMESTAMP—4:36 PM

MAGNUS: [gestures toward chair] Mr. Florez, take a seat.

METAXA: And close the door behind you.

FLOREZ: Doctor Metaxa.

METAXA: [nods] You've lost some weight since we last saw each other.

FLOREZ: Just enough to squeeze into a space capsule. [turns] Professor, I don't think we've met.

MAGNUS: [rises] We've been in the same room. Ran into you
briefly, actually.

FLOREZ: [shakes hands] That so?

MAGNUS: One of those NASA functions, bunch of government
big-wigs. The vice president was there. You gave... an
interesting speech, if I recall.

FLOREZ: Oh... that's right. [sits] Truth is, I had a few drinks
that night.

MAGNUS: You and me both. It got pretty boring, pretty fast.

FLOREZ: That's what happens when you let a bunch of space
nerds throw a gala.

MAGNUS: It becomes a science fair.

FLOREZ: Without the fun of a baking soda volcano.

MAGNUS: Well, do you recall the contents of that speech? You
didn't really talk about space. Or science at all for that
matter. You gave an eloquent... I would call it a humorous
venting session about NASA.

FLOREZ: At least you thought it was funny, I guess.

MAGNUS: I would say you came off as charming instead
of obnoxious. But it was a close call. Mr. Florez, I'm a
psychologist. I couldn't help but detect some bitterness, too.

FLOREZ: [looks down] About what?

MAGNUS: The space agency. The government. The powers that
be. Why so antagonistic when you were heralded as a hero
for your efforts during Expedition 132?

FLOREZ: Well I didn't ask for that...

METAXA: Perhaps a part of you feels it was unwarranted?

FLOREZ: [shrugs] The praise didn't feel justified. Any man could have spotted the damage. Anyone on the station could have repaired it. Kaznach was out there with me on the spacewalk. He was instrumental in the analysis. And Duvvur was the one who briefed Commander Avery. It was a team effort.

TIMESTAMP—5:19 PM

METAXA: What can you tell us about the character of Officer Duvvur?

FLOREZ: Duvvur? He— he's a good man. Very genuine. Trustworthy. An upstanding astronaut if I've ever met one. [chuckles quietly]

METAXA: [smiles] Then I trust you'd have no qualms with him as your commander?

FLOREZ: None at all. In fact, I'd have no qualms with anyone as my commander. Space is chaotic. You need structure up there.

MAGNUS: So you're no longer chafing about authority?

FLOREZ: Nah. Space is big enough for all of us.

Gabriel Florez is a humble man, prone to deflect when confronted with too much attention. He may actually prefer the relative isolation of space. A sanctuary for the astronaut to work, unburdened by the perceptions of others.

—Prof. Edward Magnus

¤

"Sadakov was right." Red's voice was confident, but his breathing was labored. *"Jesus."* Naidoo, Topfsky, Sho, and Abrams floated in a sphere around the intercom. Dixon and Sadakov hovered above like birds of prey.

Radio silence for several minutes. The astronauts exchanged worried glances. Then, like the sparks of a campfire, the speaker crackled to life. *"I have a clearer visual. Over."* It was the strained voice of Florez. They released a collective sigh. *"Three of the seven radiator panels are seriously damaged. I'd have to examine the extent, but a lot of this seems... unrepairable. Over."* The crew groaned.

"And there's something else." It was Red. *"Frozen flakes of ammonia are escaping at regular intervals. There's a leak coming from the cooling loop's pump module. Over."* Though it was softer, the crew could hear the astronaut's additional comment: *"God, it's a blizzard."*

Naidoo tried not to betray her concern. "Can you at least repair that? Do you have the necessary equipment?" Silence. "Boys, I can't hear you nod."

"*Affirmative. We have necessary supplies. With your approval, Florez and I will begin procedure to retrieve the replacement PM from the External Stowage Platform. Over.*"

"Proceed."

A grueling half-hour passed with periodic check-ins. Inside the space station, the astronauts' faces grew increasingly flushed.

"*Removal a success. Approaching leak now.*" Abrams bit his lip. The true operation began now. His mind flashed back to Florez's description of the Expedition 132 EVA fiasco. He hoped history wouldn't repeat itself. "*I'm going to—*" Florez grunted. "*—begin mounting PM onto LMC.*"

"What's Red doing, lookin' pretty?" muttered Dixon.

"*I'm assisting on stand-by with tools, dumbass. Over.*"

Naidoo's hand curled and uncurled. "Stay focused." Another hour dragged on, and the heat began to feel suffocating. The crew couldn't help but envy the two astronauts' temperature-controlled environment.

Finally, progress: "*Replacing pump module now,*" Florez announced. The crew heard him wheezing. Abrams felt his muscles tensing.

"*Damaged PM removed,*" Red reported.

"*Attaching n—*" The voice cut short.

"Florez?" Naidoo's eyes widened. "Florez. Come in." The commander actually slapped the intercom console. "Florez—status report!"

"—ow."

Topfsky laughed. "Radio delay."

"Coolant system re-engaged. Ammonia loop stabilizing," declared Red. The crew cheered. *"What was that?"*

"Radio delay, disregard the—"

"What are you doing?"

Naidoo's nose wrinkled. "I'm sorry? Red?" No reply.

"Commander..." stuttered Topfsky. "I'm not sure Red is talking to us."

"Florez, don't do it."

"Red, status!" shouted the commander.

"Commander, Florez is attempting to de-tether!"

She gasped. "What, why?"

"I am already a dead man." Abrams could picture Florez smiling under his helmet.

Red's speech was guttural. *"Like* hell *you are!"* Sounds of a muffled struggle emanated from the intercom. *"Stay. Still... No! Florez don't..."*

"I'm going to Emma." Air hissed out of Florez's mouth, and then a grunt. A warning light flashed on the console.

"He's loose." Red was breathing heavily. *"Gotcha! Okay, Commander..."* Red panted. *"I have him by the—"* Thump. There was an ominous pause.

"He's hurtling away." The words could barely escape Red's throat. *"He... He kicked me."* The Russian sounded more confused than upset.

"Red! Listen to me." Naidoo's voice was shaking. "Do not. I repeat, DO NOT go after him. Do you understand? Do you copy?"

"Icanreachhim! Mynitrogenjets—"

The commander carefully chose her words. "You. Have. Very. Limited. Fuel."

Another warning light. "Commander," whispered Topfsky. "Red's de-tethered." Naidoo lowered her head.

"Florez! I'm coming."

"Pfff...Pffff...Clifford? Pffff...Go back!" Abrams suddenly felt nauseous. He imagined Florez spinning uncontrollably.

"I'm not letting you do this..."

"Pfff...Bastard..." Suddenly, the sound of retching, then a great belch.

Sadakov held his own neck. "He's vomiting."

"Can't...Eghhh...See."

"Florez! No!"

"Can't. See."

"Please..."

Static. Then Florez: *"I can't see the stars."*

Topfsky froze, staring at the console. She shuddered. *"Commander, he... The helmet is off."*

Silence.

"R-red. Get back." Silence. "Red—"

"I can't. Florez is dead. And I'm too far."

"Have you tried—"

"Commander, I can't." Silence. So calm. Accepting.

"Abrams?" Tears gathered on Naidoo's face.

"Yes, Commander?"

"Go get Verne."

He eyed her quizzically, then realization dawned. Abrams rushed for the aft and grabbed one of the several volumes the man had left scattered about. The book's binding was splitting and fragile. He opened it without care and winced at a sudden tear. His trembling fingers held the page that fell out as he returned to the rest of the crew.

"—has been a privilege working beside you." Naidoo sounded confident even as she wept. "Abrams, read."

He held the page before squinting eyes:

'So, as I said he would, this man died in the night?'

'Yes, M. Aronnax.'

'And he rests now, near his companions, in the coral cemetery?'

'Yes, forgotten by all else, but not by us. We dug the grave, and the polypi undertake to seal our dead for eternity.' And burying his face quickly in his hands, he tried in vain to suppress a sob. Then he added: 'Our peaceful cemetery is there, some hundred feet below the surface of the waves.'

'Your dead sleep quietly, at least, Captain, out of reach of the sharks.'

'Yes, sir, of sharks and men.'

Red sighed. *"Thank y—"* The intercom speaker sputtered and died.

PART THREE

Of Sharks and Men

"The sea is the vast reservoir of Nature. The globe began with sea, so to speak; and who knows if it will not end with it?"

—Jules Verne,
20,000 Leagues Under the Sea

Sittin' in the mornin' sun
I'll be sittin' when the evenin' come...

As the ash settled, Earth was beset upon by darkness. The astronauts orbited a world that had gone cold and dead. Undoubtedly, there were infernos still raging, whole populations starving, radiation sickness devouring the masses. But the smoke plumes had ascended from the planet and expanded, covering the globe in a black shroud. From 230 miles up, the stark truth was obscured like the face of a corpse hidden beneath a sheet.

Watching the ships roll in
Then I watch them roll away again...

Abrams felt like he was trapped in the bowels of a ocean-going vessel, forced to endure the stifling heat in darkness, unaware of the world outside. Though the ammonia leak had been stemmed, preventing the continued rise of temperature, nearly half of the station's radiator panels were useless. And so the crew lived in a sweltering stupor.

I'm sittin' on the dock of the bay
Watchin' the tide roll away...

Even the constant music that Dixon insisted upon, which admittedly had been a comfort for a while, now almost seemed to mock itself. It sounded as if it had been slowed just a beat, warped by the thick air. It was enough to turn a song he once found soothing into something hallucinatory and horrifying.

> *I'm just sittin' on the dock of the bay*
> *Wastin' time...*

Abrams perceived a shift in himself. A quiet aching under his skin, a scream trapped in his lungs, a lump in his throat the size of a planet. *Three dead. Three and billions more.* He hovered, shirtless, eyes glazed, letting Otis Redding's distorted voice ebb and flow. The singer sounded half-drunk. Abrams felt woozy.

> *Looks like nothing's gonna change*
> *Everything still remains the same...*

They hovered apart from one another, not in separate rooms, but immersed in separate ruminations. Sadakov growled softly, the dark stains under his arms making him look like some sort of jungle cat. Or not. Scowling at Dixon, the man gnawed at the side of an apple, more like a hound to a bone.

Dixon didn't notice. He faced the window, his hand skimming the top of his head. He had cut a shirt into a long strip of fabric, wrapping it across his brow and tying it behind his ears to keep from having to constantly blink the sweat out of his eyes.

Topfsky, curled in a ball, scribbled fiercely at her notebook. With a crack, the pencil split suddenly in her fingers, the two shards flying in opposite directions. One projectile spiraled toward Sho, and he caught it awkwardly with his left hand. He offered it sheepishly to the Russian, who declined it with a wave of her hand, burying her head in her arms. The other shard sailed past Naidoo, her eyes following the yellow javelin as it passed inches from her face. Guilt fumed around her like a pestilence. She floated farthest from the crew, as if to spare them her affliction. The commander shook her head and retreated down a corridor.

> *I can't do what ten people tell me to do*
> *So I guess I'll remain the same...*

After weighing the move for several minutes, Abrams followed Naidoo. He found her alone, at the opening to the botany lab. Abrams coughed politely. "For the hundredth time, it's not your—"

"It *is*." Naidoo traced a finger across her forehead and down the bridge of her nose. "I'm commanding officer. I've said that many times."

"You have," relented Abrams.

"And with that title *I* accepted both authority... and responsibility."

"Lesedi, they both chose their fate."

"That's bull. *I* sent you after Red. *I* sanctioned Florez's accompaniment. They tied the noose, but I handed them the rope." Naidoo closed her eyes. "Maybe... maybe I should not be in charge."

For a moment, Abrams considered the idea. *No.* "That's bull. We still need..." He stole a quick glance out a porthole to the void beyond. "...direction. You've filled Duvvur's shoes."

She scanned the botany lab and its foliage, now brittle and brown. "A dead man's shoes."

"Well, six of us are still alive."

"My crew? Dixon's a schoolboy. Topfsky's a wreck. Sadakov is a powder keg. Sho's a mute. How can I command these people, Abrams? Where can we go from here?"

"Forward."

She sighed. "Noah... we travel in circles."

Sittin' here resting my bones
And this loneliness won't leave me alone...

¤

PSYCHOLOGICAL EVALUATION

Expedition 145
Subject: Lesedi Naidoo
Born: 4/28/94; Polokwane, South Africa

Subject has been hardened by war, though the tools she carried were bandages, iodine swabs, and medical gloves. Demonstrating extreme dedication in wide-ranging fields of study from biology to aeronautics, she remains an exemplary candidate for the upcoming expedition.

Included are excerpts of key exchanges.

<u>TIMESTAMP—1:03 PM</u>

MAGNUS: Good afternoon. Pleasure to meet you. I'm Professor
    Magnus. Doctor Naidoo, meet Doctor Metaxa.

METAXA: [rises and shakes hands] She's a medic, Eddie.

MAGNUS: With a doctorate, Stephen.

NAIDOO: I'm a medic first. I always say there's a big difference
    between working near a waiting room filled with
    magazines and working on a soldier that a magazine has
    been emptied into.

METAXA: That experience in high-stress situations brought
    your name to the top of the list.

MAGNUS: [looks down at folder] South African Air Force…
    And I see here you operated alongside the famed 2
    Squadron.

NAIDOO: [bares her teeth] Under.

MAGNUS: [chuckles]

NAIDOO: It's no joke. You ever witness the immediate
    aftermath of a 39 Gripen that was shot down?

MAGNUS: No, can't say that I have, fortunately.

NAIDOO: [shakes her head] Always a nightmare. Smoldering
    steel. Mangled bodies, burnt beyond recognition or
    dangling from the trees. Heavy ash. Screams of pain.
    [shakes her head again]

METAXA: So what would you do?

NAIDOO: [shrugs] I'd assess the situation and get to work.

TIMESTAMP—2:04 PM

METAXA: Why space?

NAIDOO: I suppose I got tired of the ground when all the action was overhead. Started wanting more than patches of sky.

METAXA: There are only a handful of windows on the station. Would you get tired of those "patches of sky" as well?

NAIDOO: [laughs]

METAXA: What?

NAIDOO: Doctor, through one of those windows I can view every patch of sky I ever saw. [grins] Every patch of sky anyone ever saw.

TIMESTAMP—2:42 PM

MAGNUS: Your air force colleagues have described you as... [squints at a file] ...courageous, confident, and extremely competent. But they've also called you stubborn, controlling, and occasionally aloof. Do you work well with others?

NAIDOO: [leans forward in her chair] I'll answer it this way. I was born a day after the first free elections in South Africa—in the city of Polokwane, which means "Place of

Safety." After the end of apartheid, my parents voted for the first time in their lives. Since quite literally my birth, my parents stressed coexistence. And I've tried to follow through on their lessons in my personal and professional life. I have worked in squadrons that spoke eleven different languages. I've saved the lives of enemies who didn't want to be saved. I can work with others.

While her career path of medic to astronaut is unorthodox, after speaking with her, I cannot see it any other way but as a natural progression. She has the education, the experience, and the temperament to meet the challenges of space.

—Dr. Stephen Metaxa

¤

"It's just not safe to return." As Topfsky spoke, Sadakov drummed his fingers against a console. "Yes, radiation decays exponentially, but it's only been a little over five weeks since the last bombs. My model suggests that levels still likely remain off the charts at this point."

"The longer we stay up here, the safer it will be down there," added Sho.

Sadakov threw up his arms. "But the longer we stay up here, the less safe we are... up here."

"There's no communication," said Abrams. "No luck in re-establishing contact. Attempting a landing with such limited information—"

Dixon interrupted, "You folks are talkin' about the whens and the hows. But *where* is also a problem."

"He's right," Topfsky sighed. "I've been pouring over satellite images for days. We have virtually zero visibility. It's like reading a book blindfolded. We don't knows who's left, what's left, where the fallout is worst, whether it's total anarchy down there..."

"As for the rations..." Naidoo began.

"At least now there's more to go around," Dixon muttered. Everyone glared at him. "What? Come on, we've all been thinking it."

Naidoo held up a hand. "Well, think again. With the loss of crew, we're still looking at about six months. But only six months."

"I would suggest that food is no longer our chief problem." It was difficult to read Sho, but it was plain to see that the gears in his head were spinning. "Orbital decay. Without the resupplies of fuel, we are unable to perform our regular altitude boosts to correct for it..." He turned to face the rest of them. "My best guess is that, before our rations give out, we'll be going home—whether we like it or not."

"An' you can bet CNN won't be covering it..." Dixon grumbled.

"How long?" asked Abrams.

"Maybe five months," said Sho. "Maybe less."

Naidoo exhaled, eyeing the air as if hesitant to tarnish it with her carbon dioxide. "Five months is a long time," she declared, hanging on each word. "There's a global calamity down there, but I prefer to think that it's not a total one. It's not a matter of *if* we'll hear another human voice, but *when*."

Sadakov shook his head. "So we have a chat with some poor Micronesian survivor with a big ham radio, what then? What does that do for us?"

"It allows us to begin to deliberate the safest landing location with available experts," said Naidoo. She dabbed her forehead with a cloth. "It's what Duvvur thought best."

"Well Duvvur is dead." Sadakov's violet vein threatened to pop out from the pale flesh of his forehead.

"So are any Earthling experts worth their salt," said Dixon.

Sadakov snarled, "Is this posturing really worth our time? While each day that passes is closer to our last?"

"Caution might prevent that outcome," warned Sho from behind.

The Russian's voice boomed. "At too high a cost! Taking a risk remains our only hope, don't you see?" he sneered. "And it's too damn hot!"

"Five months is a long time," the commander repeated.

Sadakov banged a fist against a wall and left in a huff. The remainder of the crew began to trickle out after realizing that the meeting was over. Only Topfsky and Abrams stayed behind.

They watched Naidoo exit last, her darting eyes the only sign of her wavering confidence.

"Noah... I heard something rather disturbing from Sho yesterday."

Abrams crossed his arms. "What?"

"A budding mutiny orchestrated by Red and Florez a few weeks back. A horrible accusation. Naidoo."

"Sho told you about that?"

"I'm not to tell another soul." She paused. "You don't think it's possible Red's theory was true, do you? That Naidoo killed Duvvur to prevent the spread of a contagion?"

Abrams was quiet.

Topfsky sighed. "You're the damned communications specialist, talk to me! I mean, she did originally vote to leave the station. And now she's in charge..."

Abrams shook his head. "If she intended to use her new power to force another vote, she would have done so."

"Red's point still stands."

Abrams kneaded his hands. "She's doing what she can to honor Duvvur's legacy."

"Out of duty? Or guilt?"

"Careful, Eva..."

"I am only asking questions, something we all should be doing."

Abrams frowned. "I'm going to rest."

"Wait—"

"I'm going to rest."

¤

"Don't stand in the smoke."

Abrams hovered at his usual perch, a few feet from the best view of the worst sight he could imagine. Topfsky watched from behind, startled that Abrams had sensed her approach. She had followed him from the other end of the station.

"What?" she asked.

Abrams pursed his lips, scratching at the salt-and-pepper stubble that dotted his jaw. His gaze did not leave the window. "Just something my dad used to say when we'd go camping." He sighed and swiveled around. "I was really young. We'd roast marshmallows—dad on one side of the fire, me on the other. I'd stand downwind, and the smoke would make my eyes water. I'd start to whine about it. And he'd always say, 'Don't stand in the smoke.'"

"What made you think—"

Abrams shrugged. "You can't escape the smoke down there, maybe that's it." He wiped sweat from his brow.

"Way to make childhood s'mores morbid, bud." The Texan's entrance was more conspicuous than the Russian's.

"Lots of time up here to think up memories... He was a no-nonsense kind of guy," Abrams explained.

Dixon snorted. "Least your pop went camping with you. Mine gave me similar advice, ya know. Only he slurred his words. An' the smoke came from his cigar." He chuckled.

"Classy guy. Probably died with one hand pinching a cigar stub, the other scratching his ass."

"At least he *spoke* to you." Topfsky clicked her tongue. "I didn't speak concerto, so I may as well have been invisible."

Dixon scratched his scalp. "Sounds like a dick."

"He *was* a pianist."

All three managed small smiles. Abrams realized he hadn't used those face muscles in a while. It didn't take long for their smiles to fade.

"Now they're all gone," said Topfsky.

"Good riddance," spit Dixon, but the conviction had drained from his voice.

Abrams swallowed. "Do either of you ever think about the fact that, up here, life and death are separated by only a few centimeters of aluminum?"

Dixon knocked a bulkhead three times. "Every day."

The Russian nodded her head, echoing the sentiment. "God, I need to get out of here."

"There's the door." Dixon pointed toward the airlock. "It seems like God's not paying much attention."

Topfsky tilted her head. "How's your face?"

The man's fingers lingered on the pink streaks across his cheek.

Abrams pressed a hand to the window. "Crazy."

"What?" asked Dixon. "And get your greasy hands off the glass, I don't wanna have to bring out the Windex again."

Abrams scowled, but he removed his palm. "To think that they're out there. Red and Florez. Just... out there."

Dixon flicked the stubble under his lip with the tip of his tongue. "I like to hope one of 'em deserved it. Payback for Duvvur." Abrams glanced at Topfsky. Dixon continued, "Florez was a nut job, as it turns out. And Red wanted to—"

"Red was devoted to Duvvur," Topfsky interrupted. "So was Florez..."

Dixon bit his lip. "Duvvur took what was left of Florez's sanity with him to the afterlife. If ya ask me, that bullet killed Florez. It killed Red, too."

"Florez was a broken person," said Topfsky.

"Takes one to know one," Dixon remarked, meeting the Russian's eyes.

"Well, you don't seem so broken up about it," she said, not bothering to hide the accusation in her voice.

The Texan held up a spiral-bound notebook. "I've got more important things on my mind."

Topfsky frowned. "I've been looking for that."

Dixon clutched the notebook to his chest. "You weren't using it, and I needed scratch paper. To write something important—I copied it from the log." He opened it to a specific page and handed it to her.

She snatched it away from him. Abrams floated behind her to read over her shoulder. They squinted to decipher Dixon's handwriting: *Unbroken TDRS link 02:16—02:43 GMT.*

Topfsky read it again. "What am I looking at?"

"A comms link," declared Dixon. "Right before all hell broke loose."

"You mean before the bombing?" asked Topfsky.

Dixon nodded. "It wasn't officially logged. It was in the middle of sleep period. It occurred only 42 minutes before the first explosion... And it was opened by Duvvur."

Topfsky's eyes widened. Abrams inhaled, suddenly feeling queasy. Dixon smirked.

"What does it mean?" the Russian wondered.

"I dunno. I noticed it the day Duvvur... died, when Naidoo had me send a message to NASA. Didn't think much of it then."

"An undisclosed chat in the middle of the night? Minutes before the end of the world? You didn't think much of *that*?" she asked.

"Piss off, Topfsky. Duvvur's splattered brains were on my mind. Forgive me for not turning over every stone."

Abrams considered the new discovery. "Might not mean anything..."

"Or it might. There's something strange about this—" Dixon cracked his knuckles, "—and I have half a mind to play detective."

Topfsky fanned herself with the notebook. "So now you're Hercule Poirot?"

Dixon turned to Abrams. "I was thinking more like Scooby and Shaggy."

The Russian placed her notebook under her arm, and began a slow exit. "I have to go think. I'll double-check the logs myself. Triple-check them. Right now, I don't know who to trust."

Dixon raised his eyebrows. "Zoinks."

When Topfsky left, Abrams turned his attention back to the window. Dixon said nothing for several seconds. Then he cleared his throat.

"You know, you don't have to look."

"I know."

The Texan hung his head. "I... I don't anymore."

"Oh."

"It's just... sometimes ya act like you blame yourself for the apocalypse." Dixon turned away. "You shouldn't."

Abrams observed the slow rotation of the dying world below them. "Yeah."

¤

PSYCHOLOGICAL EVALUATION

Expedition 146
Subject: Noah Abrams
Born: 7/3/96; Oakland, California

Subject seems to be a paragon of the new, optimistic, bright-eyed generation of explorers. He displays an eager curiosity, almost a throwback to the original astronaut crews. That curiosity seems to be bolstered by unwavering confidence—both in himself and his prospective crewmates.

Included are excerpts of key exchanges.

TIMESTAMP—4:19 PM

ABRAMS: Sorry I'm late, the time got away from me.

MAGNUS: Not a problem. We were just reviewing your file.

ABRAMS: [sits] Everything look okay?

METAXA: [sternly] That's the issue Mr. Abrams.

ABRAMS: I don't understand...

METAXA: [reclines in his chair and grins] We've never seen a cleaner background check.

MAGNUS: [flips through papers] No outbursts, phobias, unusual tendencies or tics, rigid philosophies, or agendas.

METAXA: As astronauts go... you're a bit of a freak.

ABRAMS: [laughs] I can work on being more eccentric, if you'd like.

MAGNUS: That won't be necessary. At least, I don't think it will. But it does pose a question, Mr. Abrams. There will likely be some intense personalities up there. Would you hold your own? Would you feel the need to adapt?

ABRAMS: I'm satisfied with the guy I am—a space nerd who somehow found his way atop a real-life rocket.

METAXA: Not yet. [twirls a pen] What concerns me, and I'm being sincere now, is how squeaky clean you seem.

ABRAMS: I... don't follow.

METAXA: Makes me suspicious. Everyone's got something in their past. Something they're hiding, or at least hesitant to be forthcoming about.

ABRAMS: I'm thinking here, I really am. [rubs temple] I've jaywalked?

MAGNUS: Stephen's being a cynic. He wants dirt on everyone.

METAXA: I want to be thorough, that's all.

ABRAMS: [shrugs] You're just doing your job.

METAXA: See! There he goes again, Eddie. Not a hint of hostility. NASA's golden boy...

TIMESTAMP—4:43 PM

ABRAMS: It was exploration that drew me in. There was a time, actually, when I wanted to be a cartographer. When I was younger, I was mesmerized by the idea of seafaring by starlight, navigators reading the night sky like a map as they traversed unfamiliar waters. The wonder of the unknown. I wanted to be one of them... That is, until I realized what I wanted to discover was beyond Earth.

MAGNUS: And when did that realization dawn on you?

ABRAMS: [smiles] It's funny you should use that choice of words. I remember the moment vividly. I was watching the sunrise. And I had one of those epiphanies. All at once, I understood that mankind had essentially finished it's journey across the planet. We were ready to look up, out, beyond.

METAXA: Very poetic.

ABRAMS: Thank you.

MAGNUS: Mr. Abrams, as a communications expert, you would control access to the station's link to our planet. The job could be pivotal in an emergency situation. Are you prepared to take that position?

ABRAMS: [nods] Each crew member's function aboard the station is vital. Any of us could make a mistake at any time. And any mistake could obviously be catastrophic. I don't intend to slip up.

TIMESTAMP—5:07 PM

MAGNUS: Have you met the other prospective candidates for launch?

ABRAMS: A few. Sho and Topfsky aren't particularly talkative, I'm afraid. I suppose I'm not either.

MAGNUS: What do you make of them? Besides their... relative silence.

ABRAMS: They're smart. Smarter than I am. They're pretty damn impressive, and it would be an honor to work with them. David Dixon, who is already up there... I know him a bit. He'd fill in any awkward silences... doesn't know how not to talk. [smiles] I'm sure he could hold up both

halves of a conversation if need be. I shook hands with
Lesedi Naidoo at an event a few years back. She seems
more than capable. She'd become commander, yes? After
Commander Duvvur and Expedition 144 return.

METAXA: That's right.

ABRAMS: Well I have no reservations about the crew, if that's
the nature of your question, Professor Magnus.

METAXA: Tell me, Abrams, how would you respond if your
crew were... unsatisfied with your performance? If they
were disappointed in you?

ABRAMS: I'm not sure I understand. They won't be
disappointed.

METAXA: Hypothetically...

ABRAMS: I will not let down my crew.

METAXA: Do you want to explain to him what a hypothetical
is, Eddie?

ABRAMS: [face reddens] I know what you're getting at, but
understand this—nothing matters more to me than
my fellow astronauts knowing that I will not fail them.
Nothing. They won't be disappointed because I won't
disappoint.

METAXA: Alright, Abrams. Alright.

Subject is fully qualified and ideally suited for the mission.
If he has any weaknesses, the only one that comes to the
forefront is his tendency to avoid the appearance of failure.

We suspect this stems not from vanity, but from truly valuing the goodwill of those experienced men and women around him. His perfectionist outlook has propelled him to make his ambitions a reality.

—Prof. Edward Magnus

¤

"A transmission?" Sadakov's forehead wrinkled. The crew had reconvened within the cargo hold.

The Texan nodded. "Unless the commander was a prolific sleepwalker, Duvvur had some covert communications."

Sho's eyes shot daggers. "If you are trying to disparage our dead commander..."

Dixon shook his head. "All I'm tryin' to do is unearth—"

"And what were you doing snooping around communications?" Sadakov's voice rumbled from his chest.

"Carrying out a damn investigation, Dimitri."

Naidoo drifted between them. "Stop bickering. Look at the link, the system that was used. That bandwidth serves only one communication purpose."

Sadakov's eyes glinted with understanding. "Satellite imagery. Curious... Topfsky has become awfully familiar with that."

The woman began to open her mouth, but Dixon answered for her. "What are you saying?"

"She made it *very* clear at our last meeting that she had been going over satellite data, David." Contempt dribbled from Sadakov's maw.

The astronauts inched toward one another. "If you're suggestin' that it was Topfsky who conspired in some way..."

The Russian's vein materialized on his temple. "Is the king of accusations threatened by one he could not concoct first?"

"Dixon, this is hardly unreasonable," determined Naidoo. "An unauthorized transfer of satellite data and a crew member who is unusually proficient?"

Topfsky was seething. "I'm *unusually* proficient at most everything, commander. You'd be surprised at what I could do."

Naidoo became rigid. "Is that a threat?"

"A fact. Commander, you're just as much a suspect as I am." Sho bristled as it became clear what Topfsky was about to reveal.

"I'm sure I don't know what you mean."

The Russian flipped open her notebook, emphasizing each line with the scratch of her pencil. "Florez contracts a mysterious illness after exposure to the blood of a recently deceased Duvvur. This baffling disease soon proves potentially fatal and, more importantly, transmissible. If Duvvur had started to observe symptoms, who would he turn to?"

"Topfsky, this—" Sho started.

"Naidoo, the heroic medic, of course," the woman continued. "Diagnosing the commander, she preemptively but violently takes matters into her own hands to prevent a crew-wide virus."

Sho raised his voice. "Commander, take no note of this. Topfsky is rattling off the unhinged postulations of two crew members who were considering mutiny before their untimely deaths. What she's saying—"

"You knew about this, Sho?" questioned Naidoo. "Florez and Red had a little plot that you were aware of, and you didn't bother to inform me?" She gestured at Sho and Topfsky as she spoke. Naidoo closed in on the Japanese astronaut. "Why were you hiding this?"

Sho frowned. "I thought they deserved another cha—"

"You thought?" Naidoo interrupted. "I'm the commander, let me do the thinking."

"Well then, think on this..." Sadakov bared his teeth and turned toward Dixon. "This is all a distraction from a disturbing truth." Dixon's lip curled. "David here has been hoarding food for himself."

Naidoo turned her attention to the Texan. "Well, Dixon? Is this true?"

Dixon balanced himself against the wall. "I've been... relocating rations."

Sadakov flared his nostrils. "Call it what it is. Stealing. Trying to keep yourself alive at the expense of the rest of us!"

Abrams drew nearer. "Let's all cool down..."

Topfsky concurred, "This is getting out of hand."

"You have no right to speak until you've been cleared of incrimination," concluded Sadakov.

Dixon's face was scarlet. "Shut up, you stupid son of a—"

"NO!" Sadakov leveled a trembling finger. "Someone should get you a muzzle. It's like you crawled right out of hell and into my life! My life... my life... In my life I have never met a more adolescent, incompetent, sorry excuse for a man. Much less be forced to share space with him!"

"You can call me whatever you damned well want, Dimitri." Dixon pulled Topfsky behind himself. "It's when ya go after *her* that we have a beef." The Texan examined his fist for a moment, before hurtling it at Sadakov's nose. A sickening crack split the air as the Russian was flung backwards. He steadied himself against a storage locker and wiped a trickle of blood from his twisted nose. With a grunt, Sadakov pulled open a locker. A crazed look came upon him, as his fiery eyes came to rest upon a glimmering machete.

"Sadakov!" yelled Naidoo. "Stay where you are." But the man wasn't listening. He was chuckling. A snigger that was distorted by his nose's obstructed airways. The astronaut removed the silver blade.

"God he's lost it..." murmured Topfsky beside Abrams.

"Everyone, get back!" exclaimed Naidoo.

Sadakov charged, propelling himself by pushing hard with his legs. He barreled forward, leading by sword point. The rest of the crew flung themselves away from his line of attack. Dixon hovered, paralyzed. The Russian howled as his blade headed toward Dixon's ribcage. With sudden vigor, the Texan launched himself above his assailant. He hit the ceiling with a gasp, then forced himself to plummet downward.

Sadakov whirled around to face Dixon again, his black mane twisting around his head like the tendrils of a deep-sea creature. He raised the machete over his head. Abrams closed his eyes in horror... so he only *heard* the metallic clash. Opening his lids tentatively, he saw that Dixon held the ends of a metal rod in each hand. A golf club.

The Russian seemed just as confused as Abrams was. He slashed again, and the club and the machete collided with another reverberating clang. The muscles in Dixon's arms strained, but he held the club without yielding.

"Dimitri..." he said through gritted teeth. "I think there's a wedge between us."

Then the Texan went on the offensive. As Sadakov pulled the machete back once more, Dixon swung his club at the Russian's right hand. Sadakov cried out in pain, and the machete tumbled from his grasp. The Russian roared, scrambling for the blade. Naidoo used the break in the battle to force herself between the two astronauts.

"Sadakov!" she shrieked. "Stand down!"

But she stepped in at the wrong time. As Sadakov wheeled around, the tip of his blade caught Naidoo in the throat. Her eyes opened wide. She gurgled, as ribbons of blood began to bubble from the gaping wound. There were a few seconds of total silence before the commander's last breath hissed between her teeth and those eyes went vacant. Topfsky screamed.

The five astronauts stared at Naidoo's lifeless body. But Sadakov recovered more quickly than the rest. He pushed aside the body and thrust himself toward a stunned Dixon. He ripped the golf club from his grasp, tossing it across the cargo hold with one hand and lunging forward with the other. As Sadakov drove the steel into Dixon's abdomen, the Texan reached forward and placed his hands around Sadakov's neck.

Sadakov gasped for air, sputtering and struggling, but Dixon refused to let go. The pair tumbled above the crew, slamming against walls. Sadakov growled and pried desperately at Dixon's tightening fingers. The Russian's face grew white, then blue. Still, Dixon squeezed. After what seemed an eternity, the movement stopped. Sadakov's arms fell to his sides; Dixon collapsed.

Topfsky rushed forward with Abrams and Sho close behind. "Somebody do something!" Topfsky shouted. "Someone..."

"No use, hon," gurgled Dixon. The machete still protruded from his torso. He tried to chuckle, but coughed instead.

"Oh, oh god, David. What did you do? What did you do?" she asked. She held his head in her hands.

"Jus' defending... your honor... ma'am," he wheezed. And then he fell limp, his smile stained crimson.

¤

PSYCHOLOGICAL EVALUATION

Expedition 144
Subject: Varun Duvvur
Born: 11/9/90; Kolkata, India

Subject exudes both confidence and humility. His intimate knowledge of the station garnered from his experience on the Expedition 131 crew make his candidacy for commander particularly appealing. The way in which Mr. Duvvur's mind functions lends itself to a leadership role. Indeed, he actively seeks advice from others while relying firmly on what he knows. Empathy is what truly makes Subject such a standout. He cares—about his crew, his family, his planet.

Included are excerpts of key exchanges.

TIMESTAMP—1:03

METAXA: Mr. Duvvur, please join us.

DUVVUR: [sits] Please gentlemen, call me Varun.

MAGNUS: Then call me Ed.

METAXA: [leans forward] And you can call me Doctor Metaxa.

DUVVUR: [laughs]

METAXA: Let's get right to it, then. You've done this before,
    I'm sure.

DUVVUR: I have.

METAXA: Good. Firstly, I would like to address something you said earlier in your career. Or rather, something you didn't say. There was a major lab accident involving an experimental chemicals program that you were selected to spearhead for a private enterprise. I'm not well-versed in the science—it's not my field—but I am aware of the aftermath. Thankfully, no one was injured. But it cost the corporation millions in cutting-edge research equipment.

DUVVUR: That's accurate.

METAXA: You were fired, Varun. But not for the explosion— for refusing to relinquish the name of the individual whose critical mistake cost the company a fortune and endangered the lives of your team.

DUVVUR: He—ahem—or she... I'll say they... made an honest mistake. I wasn't about to let it ruin their life.

MAGNUS: But it cost you a job.

DUVVUR: I landed on my feet. Look, blame is a very powerful thing. People have this tendency to toss it around like it is meaningless, but it can hurt people. I was in charge, and I took the blame.

METAXA: Would you refuse to reveal crucial information to NASA, even fellow crew members, if it meant staying true to these ideals?

DUVVUR: [removes his glasses and wipes the lenses with his shirtsleeve] I believe I can stay true to both NASA and my conscience.

TIMESTAMP—1:34

DUVVUR: The first spacewalk was like a hallucination. A
    dream. So vivid in the moment... how quickly its intensity
    fades. Some have said, when stepping out like that, they
    are reminded of their insignificance in the universe. Not
    me. I never felt more significant, part of a greater whole. I
    was one among the stars.

MAGNUS: Anything else strike you during that pivotal
    moment in your career?

DUVVUR: As I hovered, I began to notice more and more the
    imperfections. After a time, the helmet begins to warp
    one's vision. You realize you're not seeing the truest
    reality. You catch glimpses of things that aren't even
    there, just stray light glancing across the curvature of
    your fishbowl. And then you leave... before the flaws begin
    to color the experience. Before you forget the stars.

TIMESTAMP—1:49

METAXA: You are a spiritual man, Varun.

DUVVUR: Is that a question or a statement? Because you
    would be correct, in a sense.

METAXA: How so?

DUVVUR: In truth, I only turn to my faith in times of true
    desperation. When I'm weighing impossible options. Or

when there seems to be no path before me. The texts
comfort me, give me direction. They present me with
other solutions. Remind me that there is always an escape
to a higher place.

METAXA: [nods] It's good to have a cornerstone for your
mental state.

MAGNUS: Well then—only one more question, Varun. How are
you feeling?

DUVVUR: Ready for another adventure, Ed.

Mr. Duvvur is capable in every capacity and noble in his
intentions. He believes in NASA's mission, and he believes in
supporting his crew. His moral center and his willingness to
put that into action elicit the loyalty of his peers, while giving
him the authority to direct them. A leader by instinct, Duvvur
likely would be a calming influence if any difficulties should
arise.

— Dr. Stephen Metaxa

¤

Six, thought Abrams. *Six and billions.*

He and Topfsky were back in the botany lab, as far as possible from the cargo hold and the grisly dance of the three floating corpses. Abrams grabbed a brittle, graying leaf that hovered
in front of him and crushed it to dust in his hand. He started
shaking. Topfsky just stared forward, wordless, expressionless.

Abrams blinked a few times, then looked around, as if taking in his surroundings for the first time. "Where's Sho?" Topfsky shrugged. He reached for her hand. "Come on. Let's find him."

It took an hour. They searched thoroughly, but there was no sign of the third member of Expedition 146. "I don't understand," mumbled Abrams. "You can't just..." The two astronauts looked at one another.

"The airlock," they said in unison.

That is where they found him. The inner door was closed, but the outer exit had been opened manually from within. Through the airlock's reinforced glass, they could see the sun rising beyond the curve of the Earth and the silhouette of a man. He was kneeling, strapped in, his frozen arms outstretched to the horizon. It was the most peaceful sight either of them had ever seen.

Abrams stared for a long while before floating over to a console and closing the outer door. Then he blacked out.

¤

He awoke later in the same location. For a moment, in his semi-conscious haze, Abrams panicked. *Where's Topfsky?* But she was right beside him, still staring at the airlock. "Seven," he croaked. Topfsky said nothing.

Abrams reached into his pocket and felt the cool metal of the object he carried. "Eva..." Abrams finally whispered. "Eva... I messed up."

Her eyes flickered, but didn't leave the airlock. "*We* messed up. We could have stepped in. Anticipated what was to come. Somehow. Before..." She turned to face him and shook her head. "Scratch that. I saw it coming. And did nothing."

"No, Eva, you don't understand." He paused. "*I* should have seen it coming. All of it."

"What are you saying, Noah?"

Abrams closed his eyes and silently shook his head. "You don't think Duvvur sent those satellite images alone, do you?" He sniffed. "The commander needed the communications specialist." He lowered his gaze. "He needed me."

"You mean..." She caught her breath. "Why didn't you tell... Why the secrets?"

Abrams grunted. "It was extremely classified. The only reason he roused me is that he needed someone who could work the data transfer."

"What could possibly be so—"

"You don't understand." Teardrops collected and quivered along Abrams's face. "The images, what we sent down... We thought it was just..."

"What did you send them?"

"We didn't know, Eva."

"Noah, tell me. What did you send them?"

"They needed us to verify... Secret facilities. Nuclear installations."

Topfsky's heart lurched. "Bombing sites?"

Abrams slowly nodded and buried his head in his hands.

She spoke haltingly. "And after the first bombs fell..."

"The *guilt*," Abrams weeped. "The guilt, Eva..." He clenched his fist. "It ate at us from the inside. Duvvur looked for answers in his stupid little leather books. I just... I don't know what I did. I watched the fire I had set with a morbid fascination." He examined his palms. "How many lives did these hands snuff out?" Another sob wracked his body.

"But... Duvvur's murder—"

"Suicide," Abrams corrected.

"But there was no gun in the lab! You were there. We searched it thoroughly."

"It was there. The whole time, tucked away in my pocket. Later, I... I hid it on Duvvur's body before he was ejected."

Topfsky's eyes grew wide. "Why?"

"I panicked. I tried to save my own ass. Somehow I figured suicide would have led to the crew retracing Duvvur's last few days... which would have revealed my involvement in the end of the world."

She hovered over him. "You... bastard. Everything that happened to us... The suspicion, the finger-pointing... God, everything! You let it happen. For what? To save yourself?"

"If they knew... If *you* knew what I did..." Abrams motioned toward the window. "I killed Florez's wife. I killed Dixon's jackass dad. Everyone you ever knew. Everyone you loved. Everyone..."

The Russian's curiosity overpowered her anger for a moment. "And Florez's contagion? What about that?"

"I don't know." Topfsky flashed him a disbelieving look. "I'm serious. Could've contracted it from Duvvur. Might've had it long before. I just... don't know."

Topfsky was pale. "Noah... you're not who I thought you were."

"I'm not who *I* thought I was. Guilt can change a man. Seep into his thoughts. Isolate him. Take control." He looked toward the window. "Maybe what happened here was inevitable."

"Don't seek vindication. You don't deserve it."

Abrams considered his next words. "No, I suppose I don't." He removed the brass bullet from his pocket and examined it, as if for the first time. "Maybe Duvvur had the right idea."

Topfsky flinched. She eyed the blood-speckled bullet. "You know, I might kill you," she said suddenly. Abrams raised his head, but then Topfsky's features softened. She sighed. "But I'm just so tired of the dying."

They were silent. Time passed. The station continued to whip around the planet at more than 17,000 miles per hour. But all seemed still.

Then Topfsky pulled herself up. "I'm going to find a drink." She began to retreat down the corridor.

The American slumped his shoulders and stayed motionless. The Russian turned around. "Well, are you coming?"

Bikini Atoll

Dawn.

Starting anew. The world blanketed in an ashen fog. Cities turned to dust, forests leveled, seas poisoned—and the haggard man fancies himself a fisherman. His flesh is clinging to bone, ornamented with scars old and new. His hands and bare feet are caked with soil. The man's eyes are a pale green—bleary and impassive. His locks, once a stark black, are now streaked with white and missing entirely in patches, like plates of armor shed in battle. The air around him is stale. The wells of sorrow within him have long since been exhausted.

The man rubs his arthritic knuckles and removes spectacles from the pocket of his tattered shirt. The cracked lenses resemble tiny spiderwebs. The man slips them on, pausing, as he often does, to reflect back to when the lenses glimmered like opals, when the palm trees creaked in the breeze, when a man could dip his hand in a tide pool and pull a hermit crab from its depths.

The sea is a dull gray now, and its waters have significantly retreated. This can be plainly seen from the hill upon which the haggard man stands. He starts down the hill, feeling the crunch of pebbles between his toes. The man reaches the shore and shuffles in until the waters lap against his knees, creating a constant rhythm that resonates in his thoughts.

His face brightens slightly when he feels the smooth moss-covered planks below him. The pier, half-submerged in the murk, is a crumbling carcass. The man closes his eyes, imagining the comings and goings of ghosts. *A trail of gulls skimming the tide. Minnows chasing one another amid the seaweed. A hovering butterfly, its translucent wings gleaming like a rainbow.*

The man opens his eyes. Desolation. The gulls became blackened bones floating in the water. The seaweed shriveled. The butterflies disappeared, the sun that once danced in their wings now enclosed in a relentless haze.

And the fish. Before, the silver creatures could be seen darting about in the crystalline water. Now, the only place the fish inhabit are fragmented memories. Yet the man wades forward, a fishing rod resting on his bare shoulder. The dock gradually slants upward, its end surfacing. He stands here now and stares at his hook, coated in peeling rust like scorched skin. He tears off a tiny shred of his shirt, twists it into a wormlike shape, and affixes it to the hook.

With a groan, the man lowers himself, his feet dangling in the shallows. Squinting through his splintered spectacles, he grips the rod and casts out his line. His missile arcs through the air and plunges defiantly into the murk.

Though his aches only grow as the days pass and his skin sags like old leather, the fisherman is stubborn in his routine. The waters are lifeless—he knows this. He fishes not for the haul, because there is none. He fishes for the false sense of normalcy. And every day to this sunken dock he returns, angling for something that no longer exists. He shuts his tired eyes.

A sound, like the wailing of a mourner, pierces the air. His eyes open to behold a distant, flaming ball. This is followed by a violent gust of wind that whips his flowing hair behind him. Like a daytime shooting star, the fireball cuts across the sky... until it disappears with a great splash. There is a far away fizzle, and the flame is extinguished.

The man's eyes sparkle for a moment, then dim again. The silence returns. He squints into the distance, but then he feels something that diverts his attention. He draws in a breath.

No, his mind plays tricks.

Again.

He sits upright and alert now. Could it be?

The man feels a tug at the end of his line.

CLOCKWISE

Without fingers, we point.

Without feet, we run.

Without arms, we strike.

We who have faces without mouths, hands that do not feel.

We are the Preordained, and we ride the waves of time.

"The purple hood..." The words escaped the Clockmaker's lips, the man's final act in the realm of the living. That night would only be remembered as a confusion of sights and sounds, a memory fragmented by terror.

The life ebbing from the man. His breaths, shallow and faltering. The wail and whirr of the burnished, brass angels descending upon the humble home and shop. The blood on the cobblestones as the angels dragged the Clockmaker into oblivion. The steady rhythm of the waters in the Venetian canals as the angels' cries faded into the darkness. The boy watched from the shadows and remembered it all.

And then the clocks.

In a fit of madness before his demise, the Clockmaker had removed his hammer from its rack and put an end to every mechanism, fracturing their components beyond repair.

Now, the timepieces had returned. All at once. All properly and accurately wound. As soon as the cries of the angels receded, the clockmaker's shop was barraged with a cacophony of ticks and tocks, bells and chimes. The noise reverberated against the walls, an echo of a cruel, unsung hymn.

And the boy sat alone, fearing timelessness.

¤

Haggard. That sums up the man in a single word. He stumbles over phantoms in the alleyways, curses at invisible fiends. Lost inside himself, struggling to escape the swirling whirlpool within his subconscious. His mud-colored hair is long, scraggly. His skin is tinted gray. His eyes are a deep blue—black in a certain light. He carries himself as if he bears a great weight, though he wears only a stained brown robe and holds only a broken gondola oar as a walking stick.

A girl follows him. Suddenly, perhaps on a whim, the man darts into a narrow passage. She continues her pursuit without hesitation, sure-footed and swift. The alley is damp, dark, and narrow. It reeks of fish and urine, though this does not deter her. It curves to the right; she turns with it.

The man is nowhere to be found. It is as if he has merged into the stone bricks of the buildings on each side of the passage. The girl detects quiet breathing in the alcove to her left, then a glint of a smile in the shadows. Before she can react, a gnarled hand grabs the sleeve of her rough-spun tunic.

"Thought you could pick my pocket did you?" he barks, anger dancing in his eyes. "Thought I would be a ripe target, is that it?"

She does not struggle against his grip.

"I am no fool!" He spits as he speaks. "I know when I am being trailed, girl!" The flame of his rage simmers to coals when he realizes the child is not the least bit frightened. His demeanor softens. The man withdraws his hand. The girl stares solemnly upward at him.

"Look, stay away from me. Do you understand?" Perhaps she nods, it is difficult to tell. The man grits his crooked, yellow teeth. "Stay away! That means go, go!"

The girl leaves, slinking into the shadows.

¤

The man leads a simple life. In the morning, he eats whatever fresh sea produce the fishermen can spare and drinks the sweet waters of the Venetian fountains. In the later hours, he labors in the dim light of a cellar beneath a long-abandoned inn. There he tinkers and winds, adjusts and alters.

Clocks are his only companions. Their ticks are conversation, their chimes are cries of joy. He frequents the outskirts of the city, scavenging for metals and mechanical pieces in the red light of dawn. Occasionally, he convinces the blacksmith to shape a few in return for some small tasks. But the majority of his time is spent alone in the cellar, toiling in near darkness, hoping the ticks and chimes will drown out the fears that haunt him from his past.

¤

The air of the cellar swirls with dust, violet in the evening light. Rotting barrels line the walls, and silver cobwebs are strung in the corners, their thin strands cocooning the bricks. A dim glow flickers from a candle reduced to a waxy stub. Beside it lies a bedroll of sorts, crafted from rags and bits of sail from the ships at the wharf. The man sits hunched, as he always does, working into the night.

The girl stands watching, observing, waiting for the man to notice her presence. And he does. He whips around, his face a portrait of disbelief and frustration. "Wha-how did you get in here?"

She motions to the stairs that lead up to the inn. He stands, clawing fiercely at an itch beneath his beard.

"I thought... I told you," he says slowly. "Never... come... back."

The girl nods, this time he is sure of it.

"What do you have to gain from me? Do you take some perverse pleasure in watching my dismal existence?"

She shrugs, then shakes her head.

And then they simply stare at each other. Eventually, the man gives in. He grunts and returns to his tinkering. And the girl watches. She is gone before the candle's flame burns down to nothing.

And then the next night she is there. And the night after that. After a while, the man beckons her to sit closer. "Do you have a family?" he asks.

She shakes her head.

"I thought as much." He stands and adjusts the hand of one of the clocks that he keeps on a shelf above the rotting barrels. He turns back to her. "A name?"

She shrugs. The man leaves it at that.

"Well, I suppose that means you have no name. Names are useless anyway, if you ask me."

The girl points at him.

"My name?" The man chuckles. "I have no name." He runs his fingers across the face of one of his clocks. "Perhaps I had a name once, but that was long ago. I once knew a man simply called the Clockmaker. I suppose you could think of me as..." The man shivers, as a ghost of his past drifts through his soul. "No, no, not the Clockmaker. No, not that." He thinks for a moment. "Just... Maker."

The girl moves closer, eyebrows raised.

"I shape time into a physical form." The Maker looked down, his palms outstretched in the fading light of the candle. "How can these be mortal hands?"

¤

He awakens one morning to find a piece of parchment draped across his torso. Groaning and wiping spittle from the corner of his mouth, the man squints and reads the words. It takes a moment for him to remember what each symbol means; he had been taught many years before. They are written in broad strokes of red ink.

Without fingers, we point.

The Maker's heart freezes in his chest. His breathing becomes strained, and his hands tremble. He rolls the parchment as tight as he can as if to squeeze the words out of existence and shoves it into the small pocket of his brown robe.

And then he is off to the wharf—more alert than ever. Paranoid. He returns soon after, a large gray sack in his hands. The girl walks in to discover him packing away his large collection of clocks. The man does not bother to look up as she enters.

"They are after me," he explains as he fills the sack.

The girl appears truly distressed for the first time.

"They took the Clockmaker. Now they are looking to take me." There is a measure of madness in his eyes. His face grows dour. "Well, I will not let them." He slings the sack over his shoulder and walks out the door. "Do not follow me."

¤

A lone traveler in the Venetian countryside, his hands nearly white from his iron grip on his sack. He forces himself to move, fighting exhaustion. He whispers to unseen phantoms. "They will not rest, so neither can I. Time does not grow weary."

But he does, and eventually he stops in the soft grasses beside the dusty trail. He soon finds himself blinking away the bright light of the morning sun. How long had he been asleep? The man groggily reaches for his sack... and his hands brush flesh instead. He bolts upright.

"You!"

The girl sits cross-legged, staring calmly into the eyes of the Maker. "Why are you so intent on disregarding what I say? You are putting yourself in grave danger. Do you know that?"

She shrugs.

"Well, if I cannot convince you, I can only warn you of what we will face." The man removes the parchment from his robe, reading aloud the message written there. The very air seems to shift as he relates each word.

They walk along the path, side by side. Silence seems to pool around them, seeping into the nooks and crannies of the landscape. The only sounds are the soft crunch of the dirt and the shallow breaths of the man.

"The Preordained were automatons forged long ago, shaped by memory and embodied by Fate itself. They are wicked beings. Intelligent, yes, but only focused upon a single goal. All else is irrelevant to them. Life, hate, pain have no meaning. They serve a higher being, that much is clear. Who, I cannot say. Death, perhaps. Or worse."

The Maker pauses, studying the girl's face. "What draws them to me is no mystery." He shakes the sack slightly, and a dull ring and the scrape of metal emanate from within. "They regard clocks as an infringement, an invasion of their domain, and they will not hesitate to eliminate any who craft such devices. Mercilessly."

The man closes his eyes, traveling for a moment into his past. "As they did with my childhood guardian and mentor. The Clockmaker."

The girl motions to the sack, then waves her hands dismissively.

"Destroy them? That would be surrender. The Clockmaker tried. He was slaughtered soon after. Do you not see? They cannot forgive. Time can only consume." He stops mid-stride and places a hand atop the girl's shoulder. "They will not end the hunt until they have taken me away. You can avoid this madness. Leave now."

The girl walks ahead.

"So be it."

¤

During the night, the Maker is tormented by his dreams. Flashes of bronze, the grinding of rusty gears. He bolts upright, sweating. His heart beats like a war drum. The frosty morning air serves to numb him, catching the sobs before they escape his throat.

A message awaits in the underbrush, crafted with bent twigs.

Without feet, we run.

A small collection of onyx pebbles form an inhuman shape, yet one remarkably familiar. A distorted foot, its toes abnormally long and twisted. The Maker kicks the image until it is unrecognizable.

The girl. She appears behind him, silent as always. In what is either a gesture of goodwill or childishness, she aids the Maker. Grabbing stones eagerly in her palms, she begins hurling them into the distance.

It is only when the pebbles are gone that he releases a bemused chuckle that grows into a great guffaw, the laugh of a man humorless for a lifetime. Tears well in his eyes. Even the girl's lips curve into what could be described as a smile. Retrieving the gray sack, the duo departs as a sliver of sun escapes the horizon.

¤

The Maker trails behind the girl, his age betraying him at a time of utmost consequence. The path gives way to soil and stone until it is entirely eclipsed by branch and bramble. As the sky darkens, the trees transform into brooding giants, their arms outstretched, grasping blindly at all who enter their domain.

Through the heavy foliage, he manages only glimpses of the girl. Fleet as always, she dances effortlessly amongst the alders, gathering leaves and dandelions only to throw them to the air. *Such innocence,* the Maker muses.

And then she is gone. The man's breath catches in his chest as he frantically searches around him. In his mind's eye, he sees the blood. He hears the unabated lapping of the canal water. *No... No, not her!* "Take me if you must, you demons!" He runs forward. The branches scrape at his flesh.

He stops short, the trees having suddenly disappeared. Moonlight is in short supply here, the skies filled with low clouds. This is no meadow or glade; this is destruction. A force has come through here—ripping roots from the ground, snapping trunks, setting leaves afire. What remains is an ash-blanketed ruin. A dead place.

At his feet lies a discarded piece of bark. Words, now all too expected, are scrawled in charcoal.

Without arms, we strike.

It is then that he hears the quiet sobs. *The girl.* She stares out into the desolation, her lips quivering, tears streaming down her cheeks. The man opens his mouth, then closes it. Coming to her side, the Maker rests a hand on her shoulder. For what seems like an eternity, they stare into the gloom.

¤

It is difficult to remember precisely when he fell asleep, but the man remembers his dream. The fountains of Venice erupt with crimson blood, and the streets flood with the gushing red waste. He feels his feet swept out from under him, as the current takes control, pulling him through the alleys and waterways as he bobs above and struggles below the surface. He reaches for the hand of a half-submerged statue. For a moment, he recovers, gasping for breath as blood dribbles off his face.

He feels mechanical fingers, clamped around his ankle. The pull is so immediate that resistance is useless; the Maker finds himself once again thrust into a world of red. His vision goes black.

A jolt of panic awakens him. Still living his dream, the man sputters and spits, saliva cascading from his lips as if he is an animal in the wild. The Maker rises to his feet, slowly, shakily. The girl stirs, but continues to doze. The man does not wake her, instead scavenging the area for herbs. He quietly chews the leaves, letting the bitter flavor marinate in his mouth as his nerves begin to calm.

Only a few minutes pass before the girl is up and ready for travel. The Maker hoists the sack onto his shoulder. They continue their journey, knowing not the way.

¤

It is noon when they stop at the pond. Kneeling before their shimmering reflections, they take long drinks of the crystalline water. Only when the man pauses does he recoil from what confronts him when the water settles. It is his face, he is certain of that. But it is featureless, smooth, like a child's doll. He runs his hand from brow to chin, and his twisted counterpart does the same.

The man hears a voice reminiscent of his own, but darker—a whisper in the wind.

> *We who have faces without mouths,*
> *hands that do not feel.*

He kicks dirt into the pond, watching the surface ripple and the wicked image disappear. Grabbing the girl by the arm, he pulls her away. They move on.

¤

The Maker sits straight-backed, refusing to give in to his exhaustion for fear of what terror awaits him. The flame of their meager campfire dances in his eyes. As he watches the inferno lick at the air and the stones that keep it at bay, he cannot help but ponder the nature of destruction.

Time withers, time erodes. What is resistance if eventually all things give in to the current? He tosses a blade of grass into the fire and watches as it curls and blackens. *But time serves as the ultimate justiciar. It rights all wrongs, undoes all misdeeds.* The man smothers the flame, and the clearing is engulfed in darkness. This night has no moon. Will he live long enough to behold it once more? The Maker releases a melancholy chuckle. *Only time will tell.*

¤

He awakens with a start, craning his head to listen. At first he detects only the wail of the wind, but as his exhaustion fades, a subtle ticking reveals itself. The Maker jumps to his feet. Hulking above him, surrounding the man on all sides, are emotionless bronze angels, hooded in purple silk. They do not lash out, but instead beckon the Maker. Aghast, he lumbers forward. The automatons close in behind him. There is no retreat.

A cowled figure awaits him. It appears no different from the others save for its silver exterior and tattered ebony head-dress. It clenches its mechanical fists, and a searing pain sends the Maker to his knees. The cowled angel reveals his crimsoned palms, dripping with the man's lifeblood.

The man weakens, withers, falls. The silver being kneels, removes his cowl, locks eyes with him. Not eyes. Gaping, cruel sockets. Its voice is the screech of metal on metal, the whirr of gears, and the cries of the forgotten...

We ride the waves of time. Your time has ended.

¤

The girl finds the Maker curled in the tall grass. She tries to shake him awake. His body remains unresponsive. His skin sags. His hands are cold. His expression is a blank clock face.

The girl sighs. She retrieves the gray sack, tosses it over her shoulder, and carries on her way.

QUILLMASTER

The mutineers gathered at dusk, the candlelight warping their faces. The ship groaned beneath them as waves struck the bulkhead, pitching the vessel back and forth. Sheets of rain barraged the deck above. The men, whispering in hushed tones, were silenced by the slow creaking of the cabin door. A gust of wind rushed in, extinguishing several candles. The man who entered was as cold as sea-frost.

His eyes were gray like a fog bank, and his beard dripped with rainwater. A black officer's cape, a garment worth a lifetime at sea, hung ragged and moth-eaten off of one shoulder. As he shuffled forward, the man's heavy boots left damp imprints in the rotting floorboards. The mutineers opened a path for the sailor. At each candle stump, he would pause, pinching the wick and watching the smoke squirm between his thumb and forefinger.

Darkness was near complete now, save for the flicker of a solitary candle. This, the officer raised. "Those unwilling to take up arms against your captain and crew, speak now and your death will be swift. But it will be merciful." The only response came from the relentless rain. "Good. This vessel has wandered for months on end, hauling cargo that will barely pay for the journey home."

He gritted his yellowed teeth, using the candle to scan his audience. "You! Rigger monkey!" He pointed at a scrawny boy, his eyes red from lack of sleep and his flesh a sickly tallow. "You brave the lines each day to keep this ship on its course, and all the while some distant aristocrat takes home the profits!" A few grunts of agreement sounded from the men. Then the officer motioned to the oarsmen. "Noblemen and merchants recline in their homes, their coin vaults built on the backs of our labors!" Another chorus of grunts, a few curses muttered. He ran a finger down his palm. "Our hands, hardened by rope, blistered, calloused, while the wealthy man grows soft as he gorges—" *Nay!* "—and bathes—" *Nay!* "—and is served by doting attendants who see to his every eccentric whim!"

The officer raised a fist. "No longer!"

The mutineers erupted in a thunderous roar. *No longer!*

"No more!"

No more!

"Not another hungry night!" At this, the sailors cheered.

The man opened his fist, and silence took hold of the cabin once again. He spoke softly. "Let it be known that on this day, at this hour, Lieutenant Solomon Siccar of the Imperial Navy renounced his title." The sailor ripped the limp cape off his shoulder with his right hand. "Let it be known that on this day, at this hour, former Lieutenant Solomon Siccar declared war." The tattered cape glowed red above the candle clasped in his left hand. Crimson phantoms quivered along the cabin walls as the flame devoured the fabric.

The rain's assault slowed to a patter. The storm wind forced the door open once again. Siccar dropped the cape and stomped on it, rubbing the fire into the wet floorboards. "That war starts with the captain."

¤

In the violet dusklight there sit two twin peaks. They stand like black harbingers, their great masses blotting out the clouded sky like ink drizzled on parchment. At the bases of these behemoths, white waves crash relentlessly, carving twisted ocean caves in the dark stone. Between the mountains is a narrow inlet, its width and depth in a constant shifting state. Jutting in an irregular fashion from either shore is a once mighty dam, now reduced to a rusted and rotting fossil. Its cracked surface is repaired with wooden planks, its skeletal support beams reinforced with cinder blocks. An equally decrepit tower rises from the center of the structure, a plain, black banner fluttering from a flagpole at its very top.

The footsteps in this tower are muffled, uneven, cautious. A hooded gentleman slinks forward, hidden chainmail jingling under his gray robe. His eyes are distant, soulless. They squint in the dim candlelight. His face, once fleshy, is now haggard and pale. Old scars disappear in a sea of new wrinkles. His seal-leather boots are falling apart at the seams, the soles dragging behind like half-shed skin.

The man's left arm wobbles as he walks, unsteady while trying to support the candle he uses to guide himself. His drooping sleeve blows freely in the breeze, the flame in his hand creating distorted shadows on the stone bricks. His left hand lacks three fingers. The index finger and thumb clamp onto the iron candleholder like the jaws of a viper, his cracked nails whiter than the foam dancing in the water below.

The man approaches the quarters of the Quillmaster. A shabby wooden door creaks and sways upon his arrival. The Quillmaster himself sits half asleep, in near complete darkness, his elbows resting on a desk made from the same stone as the walls around him. The man places the candle in an alcove and breathes a stifled sigh of relief when the burden is lifted. He enters in silence. The sleeve of his right arm has long since frayed at the elbow, revealing a hairy forearm. This hand is intact. Within its closed fist glints the burnished steel of a concealed blade. The man's colorless lips open into a cruel smile, revealing crooked, decaying teeth.

The Quillmaster is only steps away now. The hooded man raises his right hand... and gently brushes the shoulder of the sleeping figure, who awakens with a start. The hooded man opens his palm—a letter opener inside.

"Ah! Thank you, Mors." The Quillmaster shifts in his oak chair, taking the letter opener with his right hand and blindly searching for an envelope. "Light?" The hooded man retrieves the candle, returning to illuminate a small room cluttered with papers: letters, poems, diagrams and maps on the walls.

The Quillmaster pulls an unmarked, brown envelope from under a paperweight. With one motion, the man tugs the letter opener violently, as if severing an artery. He removes and unfolds a piece of brittle parchment. The Quillmaster's eyes scan the text.

"Refill my inkwell, Mors." The hooded man nods.

¤

"Hell isn't a furnace, I tell you. Or a frozen waste." The Captain's teeth gnashed on strips of dried cod. He swallowed. "Mark my words, Hell is the open sea." Thunder rumbled outside the cabin.

The Priest smiled. "If only we could bury you with your ship. When your reckoning comes, that is."

The Captain's fingers carved trails in the pile of golden coins before him. "First I need enough wealth to afford a grave of that girth."

"Avarice is a sin." The two were silent, then burst out in laughter. The Captain slid a few dozen coins across his desk with the side of his arm—the Priest's cut. The holy man rolled one of the discs between his fingers. "A consistent supply of gold." He looked up. "Now that is something I've come to have faith in."

The Captain inhaled. "I enjoy our theological discussions."

The Priest's hand vanished in the folds of his robe. New coins clinked against old ones.

Lightning flashed, briefly illuminating the Captain's features. As the man chewed, his jowls shook like an old mutt. A globule of sea-meat escaped the corner of his mouth, splattering on the desk below. His gray hair was pulled back into a tail, so tight that his scalp seemed to be wrenched upward. This left the Captain's brows conveying perpetual surprise.

He frowned, brushing off the fish-chunk disdainfully with the flick of a finger. The Priest's gaze followed the meat's arc. "The men are upset," he declared.

The Captain sniffed. "Men are always upset."

"The thunder." The cleric was solemn now. "It has left them agitated. Left them sleepless." Another thunderclap roared, as if to accentuate his point.

"Are the men aware I have no sovereignty over the weather?"

"I should hope so."

The Captain's chair left tracks in the floor's waterlogged planks as he pushed himself backwards. "What, then, does my drowsy crew desire?" The Captain stood with such speed that the Priest retreated a step. "Warm milk? Lullabies instead of sea shanties?" He spit as he spoke.

The Priest brushed spittle off his face. "I fear they will soon be after your head." The Captain grumbled, but fell back into his seat. The holy man fingered a pendant under his robe. "The prospects of appealing to their... godliness grow dimmer, despite my attempts to keep them in line."

The Captain responded with a sluggish nod. He pointed a finger skyward. "It's this damnable storm," he agreed. "If not for this endless gale, we'd've reached port a fortnight ago." He drummed his digits on his desk. "Hrmm... By daybreak, tomorrow, bring me a list of the most vocal agitators. We'll have them dragged across the keel. The barnacles will put an end to this matter." The Captain's lips puckered around a fish head before his teeth ripped it in two.

¤

An inky teardrop forms at the tip of the man's quill. The droplet takes advantage of the Quillmaster's momentary hesitation, and it falls free to drizzle down the blank parchment. "Bah!" He crumples the paper in his hands, tossing it aside. The Quillmaster massages his temples. "Mors!" The hooded man seems to materialize out of the darkness. "Ah, there you are, dear friend. Always at arm's length, aren't you?" Mors flashes a pair of stalactite teeth.

"Mors," continues the Quillmaster, "it appears the wells of inspiration within me have dried up. Where, pray tell, is my flare for the dramatic? My instinct for resolution, comeuppance?" He gestures at the unsealed envelope and the parchment on his desk. "There are sixty-six souls on that ship for Hell's sake! All their fates intertwined like hemp rope!" The Quillmaster sighs, dropping his quill into the inkwell with a plunk. "You have always been... quite creative, Mors. What shall I do?"

The sides of Mors's mouth twitch into a sinister smile.

"Never sentimental, are you, friend? I suppose that is a luxury one cannot afford in your line of work." The Quillmaster clicks his tongue. "Yes, very well. I will give them a foray into your domain." He grips the inkwell in one hand and unceremoniously tilts it until the black liquid consumes a once-pristine piece of parchment.

¤

Siccar took a swig from a flask, swishing the vinegar in his mouth before spitting it into the sea. He watched his saliva disappear under the onslaught of white froth. Then the mutineer clutched at his scabbard and clenched his teeth as a wave of pain washed over him. The vinegar seared his gums, his tongue, his throat. It was supposed to cleanse the sores, but each swig brought their incessant dull throb to a swelling agony. For months, Siccar's only mirror had been the seawater on a calm, clear day. But for weeks, clouds had obstructed the sun, and the choppy waters had distorted his reflection beyond recognition. Still, he was confident that the inside of his mouth looked like the barnacled underbelly of a whale.

He would not force this curse on his worst enemy. To be such a skillful orator, to possess such a mastery of language, but, at each utterance, to contend with cracking flesh and bleeding cankers. Siccar had received an unwelcome lesson regarding pithiness.

"Sir?" The mutineer did not turn; he screwed the lid back onto his flask.

"Rigger monkey." Siccar's gaze wandered from the prow, up a labyrinth of vine-like ropes, and across the billowing gray sails. "News from the jungle?"

"She's still afloat, lieutenant, but—"

Siccar turned to face the youth. "I renounced my title, boy."

The rigger monkey's nose wrinkled; the man's breath reeked of vinegar. "My name is Weevil."

Siccar exhaled. "That may well be the case, but back home, you're nameless. We all are."

"During your declaration, you said your name out loud twice. Impressive for a nameless man." The boy puffed out his chest.

The mutineer seemed to grow where he stood. His shoulders arched back and his infected lip curled. Weevil returned the look, standing rigid. Then Siccar chuckled—a bitter wheeze that seemed to come from the very pit of the man's stomach. His Adam's apple bobbed once, and pain flashed behind his eyes.

"You have some moxie, monkey. But what I said still stands— we are the nameless." He fiddled with his scabbard. "Difference is, I'm making a name for myself." A crash, and a scream pierced the air. "Sounds like the captain is resisting," Siccar mumbled. He sauntered across the deck, wind whipping at his uniform. Weevil followed at his coattails.

"Sir, there's something odd. The sea—"

Siccar ignored the boy's remark. "Do you know that there's a simple secret to mastering a craft, delivering a speech, and engraving your name in the hearts of men?" As the Captain's blubbery mass was hauled onto the rainswept deck, the mutineer's voice was giddy, almost singsong. "Repetition, boy. Repetition."

Weevil was persistent. "Siccar, the water has—"

"Hush, lad. Join the others." The rigger monkey shrugged, retreating.

The mutineer unsheathed his blade with a flourish, digging the point into a wooden plank and casually leaning on the hilt. Two men forced the Captain to his knees. One pulled down on his ponytail, causing his head to tilt upward to face the mutineer and his sword. Siccar looked down on the kneeling captain like a disapproving father.

The Captain spoke first: "You've discarded your cape."

"I burned my cape." The mutineer's voice was surprisingly gentle.

The kneeling man blew a stray lock of hair out of his face. "Ah."

"We're taking command of the vessel."

The Captain swallowed. "So it would seem."

Siccar's mouth formed a hard line. The crew jeered at the Captain; a few impatient voices called to hasten the proceedings. "I may hold the blade, captain. But you are your own executioner." Most cheered at this. "For weeks on end, this crew has endured a seafarer's nightmare, all while you and your chosen cronies have lounged in the comfort of your cabins." Siccar drew his blade from the deck, resting it on his shoulder. He regarded his shipmates. "Friends, the captain has fallen terribly ill on this voyage. Alas, in a few moments, he is going to pass on. We, your grief-stricken crew, will have no choice but to claim the cargo for ourselves." Siccar aligned his sword so that its point pushed against the sagging skin of the Captain's throat. "You're turning green, captain. Is that the sickness coming on?"

A coarse shout split the silence. "STOP!" The Priest's spectacles glinted in the light of the rising sun. "Under the watchful eyes of the Lord, you shall not kill this man!"

Siccar turned his head but did not remove his blade. "Father, have you not instructed us to take the righteous path? We are only holding true to *your* doctrine."

The Priest was unmoved. "Strike down the captain, and the wrath of God will envelop you and all your traitorous co-conspirators! His retribution will be legendary."

"Well then," Siccar examined the circle of mutineers, their gaunt faces and bloodshot eyes. "It looks like I am just a poor sinner." The steel was silver as it entered the Captain's throat. It exited him a ghastly crimson.

As the body slumped, the crew stood still for a beat before erupting in cheers. Then the rigger monkey called out again. Siccar sighed and cleaned his sword on the captain's lifeless body. "What? What is it, boy?"

Weevil shuddered. "What I've been trying to tell you, sir. The sea has settled. The rain has ceased." This much was true. The skies had not cleared, but the downpour had disappeared. Siccar smiled—the expanding red puddle beneath the captain would not be wiped clean. A good omen.

The mutineer's brow knotted. "Then what's the trouble? These are joyous tidings!"

Weevil shook his head. "The surf never calms that abruptly, sir. It's a lull."

"A lull?"

A voice called from the crow's nest. "Land ho! Port side!" The fog parted to reveal an impossible black mass to the east. It towered into the heavens, topped with white at its crest. The ridges of a gargantuan, snow-capped mountain range? But an island like this appeared on no map. In this corner of the world, an isle of this sort defied all logic. Siccar's heart dropped. This was no island.

The wave seemed taller than any mountain. It eclipsed the very sun; no light filtered through its inky exterior. The great wave's colossal presence seemed to graze the cloud layer itself. As the shape barreled forward, the escalating din of its crashing breakers rivaled that of a thousand charging mounts. The black tsunami was inconceivable, wrathful, biblical...

Siccar dropped his sword and sought the gaze of the Priest. The holy man's hand shook as he removed his spectacles, wiped them vigorously with the hem of his sleeve, and carefully placed them back on the bridge of his nose. Finally, the Priest's eyes met the mutineer's. They were fearful, aghast. He looked just as surprised as anyone at the prescience of his prophecy.

His retribution. The mutineer took a swig of vinegar and let the pain wash over him.

¤

"Alright, how many do you want?"

Mors shrugs. He holds up five fingers.

The Quillmaster raises an eyebrow. "Only five sailors? Mors, that is refreshingly tenderhearted of you."

The hooded figure grunts and shakes his head. He forms a circle with his other hand.

"*Fifty* men, Mors? Fire and brimstone, man, that scarcely leaves me with anyone but the key players!"

Mors shrugs.

"I already gave you the Captain, you scoundrel. He could have served as an excellent foil to Siccar! The aristocracy versus the common man, authority versus lawlessness..."

Mors makes the sign of the cross on his chest with one of the two fingers on his left hand.

"Yes, I suppose I still have the Priest." The Quillmaster sighs. "Yes, very well, I can work with fifteen souls..." He wags a finger at the hooded figure. "But *I* select the survivors."

Mors signals his consent with a curt nod.

"Go see to the dead, you grim bastard."

Mors fades into the shadows.

¤

The wave's breaker hung above them, a horrifying white sheet so large that the final, terrible crash would actually take some time. So Weevil followed his instincts. He would climb.

While his shipmates scrambled below, the boy found himself scaling the net that extended from the crow's nest. Weevil focused only on his fingers, barely grasping the rope before swinging himself higher. He heard the yells of men clambering for refuge in the vessel's lowest compartments, but the boy continued to ascend. Fleeing to the ship's interior was utter folly—were they so eager to see themselves drowned?

The vessel began to pitch to the side while riding headlong into the base of the shadowy tsunami. Soon, Weevil was not climbing up; he was hanging perilously from a horizontal mast. With his brain frozen in fear, his body reacted. The rigger monkey threw his legs up and around the wooden pole and used every muscle to cling to the mainmast. The instant the breaker struck the ship, Weevil buried his head.

But the masts were toothpicks against the impossible wave. They splintered instantaneously, and the deafening sound lingered in the rigger monkey's psyche. For a few moments, the boy was in free fall, but, before any fatal impact, Weevil was swallowed by the black mass. Digging his fingers into the broken mast, he was whisked into the darkness. The waters sent him spiraling, tumbling, heedless of all direction.

Only one thought entered Weevil's mind as saltwater filled his nose and ears—this wave was aberrant, unnatural. The tug of the sea was hardly indifferent. It was spiteful, almost malicious. A hundred undercurrents assailed him at once, toying with the boy, spinning him around as if judging his worth, the way a prospective buyer might examine a porcelain doll.

Apparently satisfied, the malevolent entity spit him out the other side. Weevil gasped for air, and the cruel morning mist bit at his throat. Peering through narrow slits, the boy made a miraculous discovery. Somehow, by some twist of fate, the wooden mast that had served as his lifeboat had survived the tumultuous escape. Weevil and the pole bobbed in the water now, innocently, almost calmly, as the groan of splitting timber grew distant beneath them. In the bubbling depths, the boy thought he could make out the indistinct form of the vessel that he had called home. Perhaps his mind played tricks, but Weevil could have sworn he saw the flailing limbs of his drowning companions, arms groping blindly for leverage that would not arrive. Weevil watched, helpless, as the crew was dragged into the deep.

For the longest minute of the lad's life, the wave barreled toward the horizon. The darkness filtered out of the sea just as quickly as it arrived. Peaceful azure waters lapped against Weevil's makeshift craft. The boy shook, unable to comprehend.

Then an erratic series of foamy geysers erupted around him. Like whale spouts, seawater sprayed into the air as men burst forth from the abyss. Shuddering breaths escaped dripping mouths. Weevil was spurred to action by hoarse calls for aid. So he paddled, collecting shipmates floundering above the surf.

The boy counted twelve heads, mutineers and loyalists alike. The conflict was a distant memory now as survival took precedent. A few managed to climb onto the mast, riding atop the pole while clutching it between their knees. Most simply held on for dear life, taking advantage of near invisible crevices in the wood or seizing what little netting trailed alongside. Thirteen souls bobbed in the water now, having narrowly avoided their demise.

Suddenly, two new voices joined the chorus of ragged breaths...

The Priest's spectacles, badly mangled, clung stubbornly to the valley of his arching nose. Treading water in his flowing clerical garb, he looked like a blackened stingray. Weevil offered his hand. The Priest sputtered something incomprehensible, but the grateful twinkle in his eye said enough.

Siccar's arrival was louder, more frenzied. Dilated pupils darted wildly in sunken sockets. The oily ringlets that normally cascaded from his chin were plastered to his face. His bulbous, infected tongue licked the salt that had crystallized around the rim of his mouth. He clambered onto the floating refuge without assistance. Siccar released a feral growl at the realization he had lost one of his boots, leaving one foot with only a soggy, threadbare sock. The mutineer wiggled his toes in the red dawnlight, snarling again.

But then Siccar laughed. It was a terrible, guttural, humorless thing.

The Priest's shoulders heaved as he panted. "What? What is it?"

"Tell—" Siccar coughed. "Tell that vindictive prick you call a god that he'll have to do better than that if he wants to take me out." Then his eyes rolled back in his head.

¤

Damnation, thinks the Captain, absent-mindedly brushing the soft flesh under his chin. *I was right.* He peers down the precipitous drop and is greeted by an indefinite expanse of blue. The open ocean. "Died at sea, now dead at sea," he mutters under his breath. "Typical." The Captain rubs at the goosebumps that dot his arms. He thought Hell would be warmer.

He grunts and turns his attention to his immediate surroundings. The Captain stands on some sort of crumbling structure. *An oceanic dam?* He decides to look over the other side. The ancient architecture has eroded away in many places, and the gaps are filled with scavenged materials. He passes wooden planks, twisted nails, bare scaffolding. *Seems that Hell's denizens don't excel at maintenance.* The water level is lower on this side, hindered by the great barricade. In a few spots, massive cracks gush seawater—leaks that could compromise the integrity of the entire structure. Ticking down the seconds to disaster. *Alright Hell, I had my doubts, but that is fairly diabolical.*

A crunch of pebbles behind him. The Captain swivels to come face-to-face with an impish creature. The little man's face is somber and creased with countless wrinkles. He wears a simple gray robe tied around clinking chainmail. The goblin-like figure gestures with two fingers, his only two.

The Captain clears his throat. "Am I dead?" He wants confirmation.

The imp sighs, clearly tired of the question. He nods an affirmative.

"Are you... Death?"

The little man shrugs. He gestures again, then begins an awkward gait down the length of the deteriorating dam. The

Captain follows a few steps behind. They meander around gaping holes and rotting boards. Suddenly, the Captain stops in his tracks. "Are you... are you going to poke me with a cattle prod?" This garners no response. "Make me push a boulder up one of those two eerie mountains only to have it roll back down?" The imp wags a finger, but continues forward. *This ignorance is torture in itself.*

Soon the Captain notes he is not breaking a sweat, not the least bit winded. On the ship, most of his time was spent hunched in his cabin. There were days when he stood only to relieve himself. Now exhaustion is an alien notion. "Hell..." he says, then snorts. After an indeterminate period of time, the Captain steps off the derelict dam and on to the craggy mountainside. Instead of ascending the peak, the pair rounds its edge. From a distance, the mountain had appeared untouched by man. But the mysterious figure leads the Captain down imperceptible grooves in the stone, pathways weathered by footfall. *This trail is ancient,* the Captain decides, *from a bygone era.* His mouth arches downward. *How many men have trodden this path?*

Their destination gradually makes itself known. A cliff face, a table covered with a cloth, two chairs. And a man, hands clasped behind his back as he squints at the horizon. The Captain only glimpses the quill tucked behind the man's ear as he comes up beside him. The Quillmaster turns.

"I see you've met Mors."

The Captain shuffles his feet. "I had the privilege."

The man scoffs. "Everyone meets Mors, sooner or later. An encounter with the louse is less a privilege than it is an inevitability. A conversation with me, however..." The Quillmaster nods his head, affirming himself. "Yes, I daresay that's a great privilege. Everyone is guided by my hand, though very few are granted the chance to shake it."

The Captain says nothing. He opts instead to peer over the ridge. White surf crashes against the rock face far below.

"Go ahead and jump," says the Quillmaster, "if you'd like." The man sits on one of the two chairs, then continues. "You'll resume your journey to the afterlife that awaits you."

"What is this place? Purgatory?"

"A detour." The Quillmaster gestures toward the opposite chair. "And an opportunity, if you should choose to accept it." The Captain does not move. "...Or you could jump off the—" The Captain sits. The Quillmaster smiles and removes the tablecloth with a flourish. Atop rests an immaculate, porcelain chessboard. The Captain immediately notes some unusual features. The pieces have only been assembled on a single side of the board—the side of the Quillmaster. And the composition of the little black pieces is nonsensical: a queen, a bishop, and thirteen pawns.

"All that remains of your motley crew," the man declares. "Look!" He jabs a finger at a black king, discarded beside the board and hewn in two. *"This* one's you." The Quillmaster laughs, less the malevolent cackle of an all-powerful being, more the teasing chortle of a schoolyard prankster.

"Are you God?" He blurts out the question.

The Quillmaster clicks his tongue. "If I were God, I'd give a damn about morality, captain. All I care about is a good story." Somehow, this puts the Captain at ease. But the Quillmaster is not finished. "And I like a good revenge story, don't you?" He swivels the chessboard around so that the pieces line up before the Captain. The Quillmaster crosses his arms, a mischievous glint in his eyes. "Your move."

¤

The Priest examined his hands—prunes after hours of fruitless paddling. More fragments of ship had begun to bubble to the surface. Theirs was a fleet of broken doors and floorboards, snapped masts and ladders. Miraculously, the survivors stayed together—the sea was calm and the current strong. The fiercer men forced themselves onto the superior wreckage, relegating weaker crewmen to cling like barnacles or bob alongside. The Priest observed an unspoken rule: When a claim was staked, there were no challengers. Treading water left the exhausted floaters at a disadvantage—a good kick to the head would send any man tumbling back into the water. Any sense of camaraderie among the crew had joined their ship in the depths. Perhaps it was never there.

The Priest found that his gaze always returned to Siccar. The man had jolted awake not long ago. Now, on the far end of the mast, the mutineer growled to himself like a mangy dog. Siccar's eyes kept flitting to a man off to starboard. The Priest did not know this man's name, though his hooked nose was unmistakable. This was one of the nameless wretches who had operated in the darkness of the hold—counting cargo from one end of the room to the other, then starting up again. The Priest recognized the man by his silhouette. He had only descended to that gloomy place when the Captain had needed to castigate the cargo-dwellers. To remind them that the Lord could still see them in the dark.

The crow's nest had surfaced, an enlarged basket now covered in cascading streams of seaweed. The man perched within. The Priest caught whispers from the rest of the crew—they had taken to calling this fellow the Crow. With his fishhook nose and penetrating gaze, the moniker certainly fit. The other men shot covetous glances at the bird-man and his barrel-like fortress, and the Crow's position was enviable. The nest did not pitch and turn; it was dry and well-protected. The Crow had even managed to salvage an oar, and he used it to fend off men who drew too near. Regardless of the rank the man once held, poles had shifted. Power now resided with the Crow.

Siccar did not take sidelong glances at the nest like the other men. He stared the Crow down. The bird-man returned the favor, meeting the mutineer's gaze while massaging his jaw.

Suddenly, Siccar said something and slid into the water. The Priest raised his head, grabbing the boy's shoulder. "What did he say?" Weevil craned his neck, scanning the surf. "Come on now, rigger monkey, what's the brute aiming to accomplish?"

Weevil adjusted himself on the mast. "He said he's going to kill the Crow." The boy pointed. The Priest then spotted Siccar, a shadow under the waves.

"Well," the Priest sputtered, "do we stop him?"

"We? You maybe." Weevil's eyes narrowed. "Just call another damnable wave. That'll stop him."

The cleric fingered the necklace under his robe. "I told you, boy. I did not send that wave."

The boy brushed damp hair off his face. "But you called for it. Didn't you?" The Priest said nothing.

The pair watched Siccar surface. The mutineer began scaling the seaweed that draped the sides of the crow's nest. Like a spear-fisherman, the Crow jabbed at the man with his downturned oar. Siccar evaded the first jab, then the next. At the third attack, he grabbed the oar and pushed, sending the Crow toppling backwards. The mutineer used the drop in defenses to his advantage, climbing into the nest and gripping the Crow by the back of his head. Siccar's voice barreled forth, addressing the other thirteen crewmen: "See this?" He removed a large gray lump from his side pocket. "See this!" he repeated, this time a command. With his left hand, the mutineer held the struggling Crow, helpless in his grip. "ONE BIRD!" Then, with his right hand, he raised the gray object to the heavens. "WITH ONE STONE!"

The Priest closed his eyes, but he still heard the crack of stone on skull.

¤

The Quillmaster shields his mouth as he whispers to Mors. "What is he playing at?" They watch the Captain from a distance, the wind whipping at their black robes. As the recently deceased man maneuvers the little black chess pieces, a slight smile creases his lips. The Quillmaster shakes his head. "He's just allowing the mutineer to reassert his power." He removes the quill from behind his ear and starts forward. "I need to stop—"

Mors blocks his path with one arm.

"I don't understand. He's letting his killer *win*!"

Now Mors shakes his head. He drops to his knees and fumbles about on the ground.

"What are you doing now?"

The impish man rises, two pebbles resting on his palm. He begins walking up the steep incline of the mountainside. Satisfied, Mors raises one finger, then sends the pebble rolling down the slope. It skips and jumps down the rock face before coming to a gradual stop—inches from the drop-off. Then Mors ascends still further and raises two fingers. He drops the pebble and watches it tumble down. It unceremoniously disappears over the cliff's edge. The Quillmaster imagines the small splash far below. Then his features soften. "Mors, you dog. Of course! The higher the rise..." He kicks off the first pebble and watches it shrink as it plummets. "...the harder the fall."

Mors grins.

¤

Siccar itched at his sores, longing for vinegar. He barked more orders from his nest. "Now knot the ropes together. That should hold it taut!" He turned to the rigger monkey beside him—the boy had jumped at the opportunity to join the mutineer in the safety of the nest, and Siccar required a young pair of eyes. "Once again, boy. The sea tries to swallow me, it spits me out. Among leaderless survivors, I assert my authority. Now, from chaos, I bring order." Weevil nodded reluctantly.

Under Siccar's direction, they had assembled a makeshift raft. Rope was the great connector. It weaved between planks, tied oars to barrels, looped around pieces of mast. This proved a dramatic improvement—the fourteen of them were dry. Some got a few winks of sleep. One man even fashioned a fishing net.

"But we're thirsty," said Weevil. "The men will thank you, for a time. But they will turn just as quick."

Siccar's fingers twisted at his beard. "Lemme show you something, boy." The mutineer held aloft a large stick. "Know what this is?"

The rigger monkey gave it a once over. "A large stick?"

Siccar pursed his lips. "Driftwood, boy. Driftwood!"

Weevil's eyes widened. "Where there is driftwood, there is land."

"And therein lies our salvation, monkey."

Weevil laughed. "Driftwood!"

¤

The Captain speaks without looking up from the chessboard. "Explain something to me. Why a dam?" He drums his fingers on the table. "Is this simply how I perceive this place?"

The Quillmaster hesitates. "It is a metaphor of my choosing. This is an... in between place, captain. You might say that Mors and I live on the ultimate border—the line that straddles life and death."

The Captain rolls a pawn between his thumb and forefinger. "In your... metaphor, then. The ocean, it represents the mortal realm, yes? And the other side of the dam... the souls that leak through to the afterlife?" The Quillmaster laughs. The mortal raises his head. "What? What is so amusing?"

"Captain, captain, captain... The living have such difficulty conceptualizing the sheer quantity of those who came before. Have you any notion just how many lives were extinguished before you took your first breath? Have you ever stopped to think of the vast, interminable masses of souls that sleep forgotten?"

"Then the sea—"

"The sea is of the dead. The *living* are the exception, captain. They slip through the cracks for a few decades. Then Mors nabs 'em."

The Captain scans the blue plane that surrounds them. For the first time, he senses rage each time a breaker crashes to shore. He sees the churning jealousies that spiral in the murky depths. This sea was not the one he had known. This sea was vengeful.

Meanwhile, the Quillmaster removes a pipe from his sleeve. He sets a matchbox on the table, lights his pipe with a single match, and tosses the flaming stick into the ocean. The man's cheeks grow gaunt as he places the pipe to his lips. On his exhale, a plume of gray smoke briefly envelopes the Captain.

The mortal coughs. "I want someone."

The Quillmaster raises an eyebrow. "How do you mean?"

The Captain nods toward the chessboard. "I want someone, by my side. The same way you brought me here."

"I'm not just going to kill someone, man! Where's the sport in that? Where's the story?"

The Captain's nostrils flare. "That's life though, isn't it? Unexpected pitfalls. Stories cut short."

"Perhaps. But when I am at the helm, captain, every death must further my story."

"Oh," says the Captain, "this one will." He holds up the bishop.

The Quillmaster sighs, rubbing his temples. "Fine. Just... just be creative about it, alright?"

"Certainly. May I borrow that quill?"

¤

The Priest had been dreaming. The sea was so gentle that the lapping waters had lulled him to sleep. As he blinked himself awake, he recalled fleeting images that had danced through his head. Two mountains... A hooded man... A chess set? Now he returned to bitter reality: the creaking of rotting planks, the groans of thirsty men. Running his tongue over peeling lips, he soon joined their chorus. Siccar's voice boomed over them from his perch in the crow's nest at the center of the raft they had cobbled together. *Land grows ever closer, men!* Baseless optimism, the cries became meaningless blather after awhile. *Put your ears to the sky. Is that a gull's cry overhead?* The mutineer's exclamations grew raspy as even his confidence began to waver. *The mainland lies just over the horizon!* The Priest considered chugging seawater—it would end him sooner.

Then, the miracle. "LAND HO!" The rigger monkey beamed at the chance to let loose the declaration. The crew found the strength to shake themselves from their stupor, craning their necks to view the distant shoreline. *By god.* They began to chatter excitedly, their exhaustion and deprivation momentarily left behind. Men who had resigned themselves to death suddenly were glimpsing the rest of their lives.

The Priest squinted, an attempt to discern any details of the faraway coast. His crooked spectacles, coated with grime, made observation impossible. He ripped the lenses from his face and started to scrub them with the hem of his robe, but his fingers fumbled. In a moment of absolute horror, the Priest's spectacles toppled through the air and sank into the sea. The man's heart froze in his chest. Without his sight, he was useless. Without his sight...

Then something handed his glasses back. The Priest, still half in shock, accepted the gift gladly. His fingers brushed suction cups. The Priest placed the spectacles on his nose... then he screamed. All at once, massive oily tentacles burst from the sea and surrounded the crew. The great black appendages extended from the depths, grabbing sailors by their ankles and yanking them off the raft. Some men were hoisted into the heavens, wailing as they dangled helplessly. The Priest felt the air pushed from his lungs as one slimy tentacle slammed into his torso, sending him flying several feet. He caught a glimpse of Siccar and Weevil huddled in their nest, batting away encroaching limbs with the end of an oar.

Saltwater filled the Priest's nose. Once again he found himself in a world directionless and without light. He was dimly aware of the screams around him, but beneath the surf they were warped beyond recognition. Crimson blood mingled in the water with the black ooze that secreted out of the creature's mucilaginous flesh. The Priest swam desperately forward, the motion forcing his spectacles against his face. He kicked upward and reentered chaos. Tentacles tore the raft apart, adding the sounds of splintering wood and snapping rope to the din.

The Priest felt his knee brush up against something. The dripping tentacle snaked around his leg, his waist, his neck. Soon the Priest had a bird's-eye view of the mayhem as he was raised ever higher. A great hole seemed to materialize in the ocean, before the cleric spotted several rows of gnashing teeth. Then the tentacle retracted. He dropped. The Priest had no time for last words, final thoughts, confessions. The last thing he saw was the darkness of the beast's abyssal maw.

¤

The Priest opens his eyes. A chill sea breeze tussles his hair and sends a shiver down his spine. His hands reflexively go to his face, searching for spectacles that are no longer there. "You won't be needing them anymore." The Captain stands before him, arms crossed.

"Y-y-you... We're dead, then?"

The Captain puts a hand on the Priest's shoulder. "We are. Quite."

"Is this Hell?" asks the Priest.

"A detour." He swallows. "Follow me, but watch your step." They begin the long, meandering trek down the length of the gargantuan sea dam.

"Why... are we not in Hell?" The Priest looks all around him.

"I had a similar question," says the Captain. "As it turns out, from what I can gather, it does not work that way. Justice after death is a mortal superstition."

"Ah." His thoughts were too crowded to offer anything more.

"By the way..." The Captain smiles, a thin yellow crescent. "I told you so." He gestures beyond the dam. "Hell, if you want to call it that, is the open sea."

"I told you so? Captain, I just died!"

The Captain winces. "Yes. Sorry about that."

"Well, I suppose I appreciate your... Wait, are you sorry *for* me, or is that an *apology*?"

The Captain stops in his tracks. "I, um... How to best phrase this? I... killed you."

The Priest knits his brow. "I do not understand. It was the kraken, this monstrous, tentacled nightmare..."

"A figment of my imagination. I was told to be creative."

"What are you talking about?"

"This... place... is the realm of a storyteller. Fate's scribe, you might say. He has given me what is apparently a rare opportunity. A chance to write my own vengeance. Poetic justice, my friend."

The Priest glowers. "Friend? You took my LIFE! I'm not your... your... your plaything!"

"Understand that—"

"I mean, my god! Hundreds of razor-sharp teeth tore me to bits!"

"A flourish, perhaps, but it was necessary to—"

"Have you any idea the toll an experience like that has on one's psyche?"

The Captain snarls, grabbing the Priest by his collar. "I had my throat slit open by a man I thought I trusted. I am not exactly feeling chipper either!" This silences the Priest. "Look. You were going to die anyway. The entire crew is fated to die, or so the Quillmaster says. But I needed you by my side now."

"W-why?" the Priest sputters.

"Because I have concocted a plan, and your assistance is crucial."

"A plan?"

"Yes. To circumvent fate and cheat death, all in one fell swoop."

The Priest scratches his chin. "That is ambitious, even for you."

"Do we have an accord?" asks the Captain.

The Priest shrugs. "Do I have a choice?"

The Captain begins strolling forward once again. "Good," he says without looking back. "Because these old bones have a few good years left in 'em."

They do not speak again until they round the mountainside. Two figures await them. The first is short and stooped. His cowl only partially obscures pale, wrinkled features. The other is taller, more youthful. One hand behind his back, he extends the other toward the Captain. "Oh, here you are." The Captain carefully removes a quill from his pocket and places it in the man's outstretched hand.

The Quillmaster slides the feathered pen behind his ear. "That tentacled beast, quite exciting! A bit derivative, but exciting! Don't you agree, Mors?" The impish man nods.

"See, Mors?" the Quillmaster continues. "Taking a step back and letting a mortal conduct affairs has thus far proven a rewarding experiment." This time, the imp's mouth forms a grim line. The Quillmaster's eyes meet the Priest's. "Allow me to introduce myself. I am the Quillmaster."

The Priest cocks his head. "A personification of fate?"

The Quillmaster frowns. "I don't like your friend, captain. He takes the mystery out of everything."

"Forgive me," says the Priest between clenched teeth. "I am not in a riddle-solving mood."

"Yes, yes, of course. This all must be rather overwhelming. A priest, his preconceptions about life after death undermined in an instant."

"Quillmaster, I presumed nothing. And, if I'm being honest, I have always feared the existence of a Hell because I figured it was my destination."

The personification of fate grins. "Well, mortals, it has been a grand time, but your little game of revenge is drawing to a close." He motions toward the chessboard. "A queen and a pawn are all that remain... and they have just reached dry land."

¤

The crow's nest slid onto the sandy shore, tipping over and sending Siccar and Weevil tumbling onto the beach. They each spat out mouthfuls of sand. Weevil slicked back his hair, still black from the monster's oil-like goo. The pair panted for a long while. Siccar coughed, then gasped in pain. The mutineer groaned as he stumbled to his feet, retrieving the oar from the overturned nest. The oar was splintered now, snapped in two. Siccar threw the shorter side to Weevil, who caught it awkwardly in his left hand. Using the remnants of their oar as walking sticks, they made their way inland.

"Must be... freshwater... somewhere," said the mutineer. The boy nodded. They refused to acknowledge the dozen men they had abandoned to the tentacled terror. They soon lost sight of the sea as they disappeared into the dense foliage of a tropical forest. Unseen creatures called from above the canopy and slithered in the underbrush. The pair trudged ahead anyway, for the sound of running water banished all other thoughts. Siccar and Weevil burst into a small clearing and were greeted by the sight of a gurgling creek. They cupped their hands and lapped greedily at the fresh water.

After several minutes of indulgence, Siccar leaned his back against a log and lazily fanned himself. "We are survivors, boy. Remember that. Drink up now, rest if you can. Soon we will be off again."

Weevil, still on his knees, raised himself up. "And where will we go?"

"I intend to follow the creek downstream. One would hope it is a tributary that flows into a greater waterway. Where there is a river, there is civilization."

The boy stood, driving the end of his walking stick into the dirt. "Why should I follow you any longer?" he asked. "I could hike upstream, to the source of this water. A spring, most likely. Or I could follow the coastline, avoid the dangers of the jungle."

"A monkey shirking the jungle, don't be ridiculous."

"Insulting me will do you no good." Weevil batted at a bug near his ear. "We're castaways now."

Siccar rose. "We were always castaways, boy. Tossed out by the elites. Discarded like trash and left to fend for ourselves in the real world. Castaways—"

Weevil spit. "I am no longer moved by your pretty words, Siccar."

"Fine. Here's why you will follow me. I am all you have. Another man increases your chances of survival twofold. And, damnation, I am the reason you are alive right now. Had I chosen, say, to not let you join me in my nest, you know where you are then?"

"I—"

"You're sitting on the seafloor, dissolving in the stomach of that monstrosity with the rest of that sorry lot. You owe me your life, boy. I will not allow you to shrug off a debt like that."

They slept in the mud beside the babbling brook and awoke sticky with sweat. The air was thick here; Weevil felt that he had to remind himself to breathe. The pair drank their fill as the sun rose, then embarked on a journey following the creek downstream. The jungle was not accommodating. Vines coiled around branches like serpents and swayed ominously. Whispers were carried on the leaves at each footfall, heralding their arrival. Humming insects flitted between them, drawing blood and zipping away. Travel was slow-going. They walked several miles.

"The trees are thinning up ahead," Siccar declared. "If our luck stays with us, it could be a settlement."

Weevil's stomach growled. "Or a watering hole. An abundance o' wildlife."

Siccar's eyes instinctively turned to the end of his walking stick, its pointed end reminiscent of a spear. "Keep your eyes open for anything that'll go down without coming back up the same way."

When they broke through the treeline, their hearts dropped. The creek did, in fact, flow into a larger body of water—it filtered into the ocean. Another beach stretched before them. Weevil fell to his knees. "It's an island. This whole jungle, it's a damnable island!"

¤

The Captain locks eyes with the Priest, but speaks to the Quillmaster. "I need to stretch my legs," he says slowly. "Think a moment before I strike the final blow."

The Quillmaster spins his quill between two palms. "Hmm. Yes, very well. But don't linger. I will not allow the mutineer and monkey to evade their fates for much longer. Giving them hope is all well and good, but there comes a time where it all must be over and done. You both move on to your unenviable afterlife, I return to my fated task. Good? Good." The Captain rises and heads back in the direction of the dam, disappearing around the mountainside.

The Priest remains reclined in his chair. Neither the mortal nor the immortal speak for many minutes. Finally, the Priest: "You know, I did not think I would perish so soon."

"Very few men expect to die." The Quillmaster chuckles. "But there is an unwritten contract, isn't there? I mean, there is a reason they call it your 'lease on life.' Life is the merchandise, the price is its inherent impermanence."

The Priest shakes his head. "If only we were told the time we had left the moment we entered the world. Remove that ambiguity."

"Where is the thrill in that?"

"But why must something as beautiful as life come to a close?"

"Because everything is cyclical, priest. Everything." The Quillmaster sighs. "Here, would a smoke make you feel better? I have an extra pipe on me." He withdraws two pipes from his robe, handing one to the Priest, who accepts it after a moment's hesitation. The Quillmaster reaches into his pocket, then removes an empty hand. He arches an eyebrow and pats himself down. "Well... that's strange." He searches under the table, the chairs, the chess set. "Where... is... my matchbox?"

"So, Quillmaster, what you are saying is that everything has an inevitable end?"

"Well, I... I... Do you smell something?"

"Everything has its end, Quillmaster." The Priest relishes the bewilderment in his eyes.

The Quillmaster rises shakily to his feet. There is smoke in the sky. He clenches his teeth. "Hell." He walks to the cliff's edge and looks toward the sea dam, or what once was the dam. Now, it is a brilliant wall of orange flame.

"The place was a tinderbox," says the Priest. "The captain and I figured it was time the line between life and death went up in smoke." The Quillmaster seethes. "So the captain swiped your matchbox—" Ear-splitting booms shake the mountain's foundations as cracks appear across the dam's surface, spewing ocean water. "—and killed me to be your distraction."

The Quillmaster's face is blood red. His hands form fists. "Do you know what you have done? You reprobates have put your grubby mortal fingers on the scale, disrupted the natural order. Do you know how much *time* it'll take to rebuild?"

The Priest smiles. "See, that is the difference between us. You've got plenty of time. I, on the other hand, mean to enjoy mine while it lasts." The dam collapses behind him. Huge flaming chunks fall into the sea, sending pillars of smoke skyward from the sizzling aftermath. Water rushes over the barrier, until the entire structure is overtaken.

"I'll..I'll..."

"What? Kill me?" asks the Priest. "No need." Then he steps off the cliff.

¤

Siccar squatted beside their campfire, using a jagged rock to whittle the sharp end of his walking stick into a fine point. The fire spit red sparks every so often, but the mutineer sent them tumbling away with a puff of air. Weevil scowled some distance away, sitting cross-legged in the darkness, staring at the spot where the pale moon was reflected on the ocean's surface. Siccar examined his spearpoint with one eye closed. He stood, holding the spear with both hands. "I am going back into the jungle to hunt. Keep the fire burning so I know where to return."

Weevil spit. "It is the middle of the night. You're more likely to be hunted yourself."

Siccar pointed to the full moon. "I have all the light I need."

"You're a fool."

The mutineer began walking inland, toward the trees. "I have a feelin' in my gut, monkey. Death is in the air." He turned around. "So—"

"So how about I douse the flames after you've gone, huh? How about you scamper off into that jungle and don't come back, huh? You're an inhuman scoundrel, but somehow I'm the monkey?" Then the boy began to cry.

Siccar growled. "You are weak!" he snarled. "We. Are. *Survivors.*" The man stepped toward Weevil. "If you continue to refuse to pull your weight..." He leveled his spear at the boy. "Well, there are other ways you can be useful." Weevil continued to stare at the sea, eyes wide. "What in damnation are you looking at, boy?" Weevil did not respond, so Siccar turned his head.

The water had began to bubble where the moon was mirrored on the waves. A great mass gradually emerged from the sea. The mutineer gripped his spear tightly, thoughts returning to the tentacled beast that had nearly taken his life. But this was no creature. It was a ship. It was *their* ship. First the prow revealed itself, the mermaid on the front immediately familiar. Then three great masts rose from the waves, complete with billowing sails dripping in saltwater. The white moonlight made the ship appear almost spectral, the soft glow imbuing the craft with an unearthly power. Finally, Siccar spotted the vessel's crew. Impossible, and yet there they stood—manning the gunnels, tugging the mainsheet, swabbing the deck as if nothing was out of the ordinary. The crew that was swallowed by the sea lived again. Unscathed. And they were barreling full speed toward the shore.

Voices carry easily over water, and the voice that rang out was so impassioned, so incensed, so *loud*, that the mutineer knew immediately to whom it belonged. "LIEUTENANT SOLOMAN SICCAR, YOUR RECKONING HAS COME." Suddenly, Siccar's face paled, whiter than the moon. It couldn't be. It was impossible. He had driven a sword through the man's throat. He had witnessed the gurgle of death's finality. He had left bootprints in the man's blood. And yet the Captain's laughter was carried across the waves.

"Quick, boy," sputtered Siccar, remembering his companion, "douse the flames." But the rigger monkey was grinning from ear to ear. The mutineer shook himself and forced his body to run to the campfire. He frantically kicked sand into the tendrils of flame. Meanwhile, the ship had stalled in the shallows near the shoreline. The anchor fell from the vessel's side and made a great splash. And—no, his eyes must have deceived him—was that a figure sliding down the anchor's chain? Siccar held his spear defiantly, but began to inch back toward the jungle.

Then a man crawled from the sea onto the sand. His gray hair was pulled back in a tight tail. Water dripped from his face and his clothes; seaweed dragged behind him like strips of an old green cape. The Captain was unmistakable, his laughter haunting.

Siccar opened his mouth to speak, but all that came out was a whimper.

The dead man stood tall on the beach and clasped his hands behind his back. "That's right, traitor. I'm quite well, thank you. Air fills these lungs, and blood flows through these veins."

Siccar did not hesitate. He hurled his spear with all the ferocity he could muster. It spiraled through the air and impaled the Captain in the center of his chest. The dead man was driven backward, but he did not cry out in pain. He did not even blink. He simply looked down at the wooden shaft protruding from his torso and clicked his tongue. With a tug, the Captain removed the weapon and tossed it into the sea. No blood spilled onto the sand. Siccar staggered. There was not even a wound.

The Captain clapped slowly. "Good aim, Siccar. But Death is temporarily indisposed."

"How?" asked Siccar, aghast.

The Captain just grinned. He turned to the boy. "Weevil, I've pardoned every mutineer. Well, everyone but one. Will you pledge your loyalty and rejoin my crew? I need a good man to brave the lines." The boy nodded emphatically, running up to take his place alongside the dead man. "Excellent. If the winds favor us, we should reach port in a few days. Swim over now, boy. The crew'll pull you up." Weevil nodded once more, shot

Siccar daggers, then began swimming for the vessel bathed in moonlight.

Now it was only captain and mutineer. "I went to Hell and back just for this moment," said the Captain. His eyes gleamed as he shouted at the heavens. "How's this for your revenge story?!"

"Just kill me, apparition," pleaded the mutineer.

"No. If I were to kill you, I would see you again. The walls that keep the dead from seeping into the mortal realm have been removed, for a time." The Captain sighed. "No. I am not going to kill you. Your punishment is something far worse. I am going to leave you to your fate."

Siccar's brow creased. "I... I do not understand."

"Goodbye now." The Captain patted the traitor on the shoulder, turned around, and walked back into the sea.

Moments later, Siccar watched the ship disappear into the darkness.

¤

Mors and the Quillmaster sit, legs dangling over the edge of a bluff overlooking the sea. The latter holds a chess piece in one hand, a quill in the other. He exhales, quill pressed against the bridge of his nose. "I wonder who writes *our* fate," he says, at last. Mors shakes his head and shrugs. The impish man points to the smoking sea. "I will not seek retribution," declares the

Quillmaster. "I am more impressed than angry, really. Perhaps..." He examines the chess piece. "Perhaps we have underestimated our pawns. Could it be that some are fated... to cheat fate?"

Mors shrugs again.

The Quillmaster tosses the chess piece over the precipice. He examines the quill for a moment, then places it behind his ear and stares out toward the endless sea, black as ink.

ADRIFT

Each step is an effort. As the man walks down the passage-way, the magnets built into the soles of his boots cling to the metallic floor. He is escorted by two uniformed guards with placid, nearly disinterested faces.

The prisoner shuffles forward, his ankles chained. Although he is thankful to have his hands free, the jagged red scars that dance across his wrists remind him that he is no stranger to shackles. Not that any restraints are necessary. He has nowhere to go.

The guards bring him into a room and seat him across from a brooding figure. The differences are small but noticeable enough—the sagging flesh, the slits for eyes, the folds of his upper nose. He is no Human, but a Swyriak like the guards who stand on either side of him. "Derek Dugall," the figure snarls. "Can't escape trouble, can you?"

"I like to think I can escape anything."

"That is the problem with you rebels. You like to think." He reaches to retrieve a file and clears his throat, his eyes never leaving Derek's. "Ah, here we are. Where should I begin? Vandalism, theft, ice smuggling, treasonous acts against the Swyriak Consortium..."

"Against the orchestrators of a genocidal coup..." Derek interrupts.

"...selling unregistered weaponry, fabricating security-clear-ance data, trespassing in restricted zones... Should I continue?" When he receives no response, he removes a piece of paper from the file and pushes it towards Derek. "Let's keep this simple, Dugall. I am the Warden. You are my prisoner. Do you know what this is?" He places a stubby finger atop the document.

"Should I?"

"Orders from Highlord Pkarr. Orders that allow me to immediately place you in solitary confinement." Derek winces. In the past, he had relied largely on the help of other prisoners to escape difficult situations. Solitary did not bode well.

"I have found my way out of confinement before."

"I am aware of that. But you have yet to see my facility in all of its glory. Come along." The Warden abruptly stands, his steel chair creating an ungodly shriek as it scrapes against the floor.

"If I were to follow you, I'd prefer the ability to walk freely."

"I am a reasonable man, Dugall." He nods his head almost imperceptibly, and the guards unchain Derek's ankles. "But do not allow this small freedom to fool you. There are no free men here."

The Warden has an unsure gait, as if his feet are making one decision and his mind another. Soon, he stops, rapping his knuckles on one of the rough stone walls. "You were unconscious during your arrival here, so allow me to enlighten you: The bulk of this prison is constructed within this asteroid, the largest in the sector."

"A waste of space," Derek mumbles.

"It used to be a mine." The Warden runs his palm along the space rock as he continues down the passage. "It had a massive ice yield. Miners from all over the Swyre Cluster made their way here. They were likely responsible for a good portion of the oxy you're breathing right now."

"And when the ice was depleted?"

"The miners departed, as miners do. Nerro Alpha, the asteroid, was abandoned, useless."

"And I suppose the Swyriak deemed it suitable accommodations for common criminals like me?"

"Common? Hardly, Dugall. You are a threat to the security of the Cluster, a danger to the people."

Derek's face grows red and he nearly lunges at the Warden. "I fight *for* the people!" he spits.

The guards flinch, but the Warden waves them off. "You Humans are feisty ones. It will give me great pleasure to observe how quickly your defenses crumble, to watch your convictions wither away. It happens to all who are sent to me. Their eyes glaze over. They start to twitch and babble. The stronger the will, the harder the fall."

They arrive at what appears to be an airlock. The Warden taps his chest, and a transparent material emerges from his collar and sleeves, molding to the shape of his head and hands. A guard taps Derek's chest, and he, too, is immediately wrapped in a form-fitting, temperature-controlled environment. He can feel the oxygen entering his lungs. Sealed from the universe, he shivers at the alternative.

As a child, he had heard stories. Exaggerated tales, perhaps, but he had learned long ago that all yarns were layered with bits of truth. In the Years of Mourning, during the centuries after the Interplanetary War, survivors began to reestablish order—attempting to live atop the small fragments of what was left. These were mere crumbs in space, the remains of an era that would soon fade into myth and rumor. These budding civilizations thrived on efficiency, conservation, and zero tolerance for unlawfulness. Without supplies to construct adequate prisons, they found a cruelly simple solution: Banish criminals to eternal darkness. No heat. No oxygen. Unconscious in a matter of seconds. Dead soon after, their corpses doomed to forever occupy the vast nothingness. Some found it humane; others regarded it with horror. The High Magistrates in Asterisk eventually outlawed the practice, but marauders and extremists that plague this part of the cosmos still used this method of execution. Looters continued to discover lifeless bodies in the void. Derek rubs his temples, thanking Aster he isn't one of those bodies. At least, not yet.

The Warden senses his worry, but misinterprets it. His gruff voice sounds in Derek's ears. "The magnets in your boots will keep you firmly attached to the outer shell of the prison. Don't summon any heroic notions." His noses twitch. "Putrid, stale oxy."

The Swyriak presses a button to open the airlock and, without hesitation, steps out onto a platform leading into the black expanse. Derek follows, far less confident. Immediately, he notices the slow movement of the asteroid into which the facility had been built. The Warden reads his thoughts. "Purposeful rotation. It allows for more expedient arrival..."

"And departure," Derek adds.

The Warden releases a twisted laugh, and his four nostrils flare. "You still don't understand, do you? The prisoners here are of a different sort. Enemies of the Consortium. Treasonous scum. Agitators. So we use isolation to diffuse potential threats. Total isolation." He opens a panel that blends into the rocky exterior and presses a few buttons labeled in Swyre Script. Derek squints as a distant object suddenly rushes toward them.

"Your new home," the Warden grins.

Moments later, an asymmetrical space rock no bigger than an escape pod approaches the platform. "Nearly one hundred of these cells—we call them Pebbles—orbit our prison. We use magnetic attraction, you see. Repurposed mining technology. We have the ability to increase and decrease the pull in order to draw the Pebbles in and send them back out. Ingenious design."

The Warden makes his way toward the end of the platform. He turns to find Derek staring at him. Again, he seems to sense his thoughts. "Do you actually think you are the first person to ponder pushing me off this platform, Dugall. The computer systems would be alerted, the airlock sealed, and you'd be left to die with me. I can assure you that asphyxiation is an unpleasant ending. I've watched it happen."

The Pebble silently docks at the platform's edge, and the Warden turns a wheel attached to its hatch. It opens to reveal a bleak interior. Stone walls and ceiling. No windows. "You will have only a bed, a book of my choosing, and a bodily waste deposit. You will be pulled in once a day for oxygen renewal and to retrieve your nutritional supplement injection."

Derek's eyes widen. "Injection?"

"Get used to a life, such as it is, of bare minimums. Hunger is merely a state of mind." The Warden motions for him to enter the Pebble. He doesn't. The Swyriak scowls. "You brought this on yourself, Dugall."

"How so? By defending the rights of the people?"

"Ruma frowns on sinners and chaos brewers."

"A god-fearing man." Derek slowly shakes his head. "That explains the cruelty." He approaches the Warden and looks him in the eye. "Are you aware that your Ruma was a major inspiration for the Interplanetary War all those centuries ago? Of course you aren't. You interpret your holy text to your benefit, ignoring the hypocrisy, the brutality..."

The Warden holds up a hand to silence his prisoner. "Ruma shall arrive in a blazing chariot of rust and bone, clothed in radiance begot from the heavens, heralded by black-winged cerulean revenants of a forgotten time..." He shoves Derek into the cell.

"This is madness!" Derek shouts.

"Oh, no," the Warden smirks. "You'll discover madness soon enough."

¤

Isolation is punishing. The weeks and months drag on endlessly, yet life becomes a challenge of minute-by-minute survival. He begins to sense a competition within himself. Which will waste away faster—body or mind? He moved through a series of psychological stages. First, a brief phase of boredom, followed by a long stretch of anger. By now, his knuckles are scabbed; the rock walls remain unscathed. Then came a powerful craving for interaction, for any conceivable distraction from the lonely silence. A real meal. Discussion of any kind. Anything. Soon, regret, along with constant musings on the what-ifs of his situation.

What if he hadn't left his Asterisk home to negotiate a trade agreement between the Asteri and Swyriak? *It was supposed to be a simple mission—a simple trade mission.* What if he hadn't been "provisionally detained" just after Pkarr's military coup, an unofficial hostage? When rebels stormed the newly designated seat of power, Derek had been freed and offered a choice. What if he hadn't opted to join the rebellion? What if his successful raids of supply ships and command posts hadn't turned him into a symbol of resistance, his participation attracting disparate allies coalescing around a purpose, standing up for a cause?

He glances at the low stone ceiling; now he can barely stand up at all. He finds himself slipping into a final stage—retreat within himself, deeper than he realized he could travel, a tomb of his own making. A single object—one that he had long disdained—allows a tenuous grip on reality: the poetry and parables in the Faith of Ruma's holy book, the *Rumalacon*. *A book of my choosing*. Derek delights in letting his eyes roam the pages as he wanders the passageways of his mind...

The concluding hymn on the volume's penultimate page particularly captivates him, not for its message so much as its elegantly crafted prose—or perhaps because he can almost hear the Warden's voice echoing between his cell walls.

> *Give thanks to the eternal one,*
> *He who kissed the stars and kindled the sun.*
> *Give thanks to He who brought forth our being,*
> *He who allowed the gift of seeing.*
>
> *Alas, alas, for the sin of the Six,*
> *who reveled in rage and took pleasure in tricks.*
> *We who quenched Aster's flame once new,*
> *and left the planets far askew.*
>
> *We embroiled in petty war,*
> *drowning in conflict and blinded by gore.*
> *Repent, repent, before too late,*
> *when He returns with our mortal fate.*

Atop a throne of bone and dust,
wielding a sceptre of iron and rust.
Heralded by revenants, cerulean and winged,
bearing horns of ice and lyres stringed.

Shadows of the black,
hunters of the pack.
Ruma, one day, will return,
but now we wait, we wait and yearn.

Eyes closed, he thumbs the pages, when he suddenly feels the familiar lurch of his Pebble, signifying that they are drawing him in for another injection. Derek despises the after-effects of the injections—a sour taste on his tongue, a tightening of the muscles in his limbs. But it serves its purpose. Derek is never physically hungry, only... empty. And his cell is equipped with an ever renewed water supply, so his thirst is satisfied.

But it is a thirst for contact that it truly satisfies. His brief interactions with others give him fleeting moments of purpose and clarity. Derek eagerly awaits the guards with their needles. The brief interactions have kept him sane this long—at least, he thinks so.

This time, he is startled by a sudden crackling from the ceiling—from a speaker that he had long thought defunct. He would have jumped, had his boots not stubbornly clung to the floor. Moments later, a distorted voice: "This is Commander

Ravere of the Swyre Rebel Army." *Ravere*... the name sparked what was by now only a vague memory. "We have seven fully-equipped Kumarri warships surrounding your facility. We demand immediate surrender of all weaponry and supplies, as well as release of the Human, Derek Dugall. Failure to comply will result in total..." More crackling, then silence.

Derek feels a smile creep to his lips, but it fades. He has become so accustomed to life in his Pebble that the prospect of change feels oddly discomforting. His cell is about to dock. Engaging the air-tight seal around his head, he grabs the *Rumalacon* and presses it into his torso. Derek pricks his ears, awaiting a response.

He pictures the Warden, startled from his slumber, hastily putting on clothing, rushing to the communications floor. For the first time in months, Derek laughs. The Warden would be forced to broadcast on all speakers. Ravere chose the frequency wisely, so that all the prison's inhabitants would bear witness to the surrender. But there is no surrender.

Instead, there is color and chaos, as one side of his cell explodes into fragments, revealing darts of red and white piercing the blackness. The prison is firing on the rebel ships. And then a massive yellow flash bursts from the largest ship. Seconds later, the asteroid explodes in a dazzling display of silver. Then Derek is spinning, spinning, his Pebble having been propelled outward by the force of the blast. He notices the whiteness of his hands—one clinging to his cot, the other to his book. Then all is black.

¤

Derek's training in planetary orienteering hadn't prepared him for *dis*-orientation. As the floor becomes the walls, ceiling, and floor once more, he finds it nearly impossible to manage his half-processed thoughts. The magnets in his boots have ceased functioning. The oxygen supply in his headshell is surprisingly stable, but for how long? And how long was he unconscious? How far has he traveled?

His book is gone.

For a moment, Derek considers escaping, too, through the hole in the side of his Pebble, bordered by twisted steel, where a large portion of the wall has been torn away. But then he re-alizes the absurdity of the notion. Escape where? If the endless darkness of space is freedom, Derek much prefers—

Suddenly, he slams into the metal-rock ceiling. He feels something crack in his wrist, as he uses his good hand to again grab a leg of his cot. Dazed, in pain, he tries to reorient himself, focusing only on his breathing, heavy and strained, hoping to approach the indifferent state of mind he had discovered during his isolation. Or perhaps re-discovered. Upon first joining the rebellion, he had volunteered to treat injured warriors in a medical ward on Terranoda Prime. It was brutal work. Due to limited medical supplies and staff, Derek was constantly confronted with life-and-death priorities. He assessed each situation with professional detachment, only allowing emotions to engulf him when he was off duty. The more the casualties mounted, the more he wondered if it was sacrifice for a lost cause.

Lost. Derek realizes that the force that had thrown him upward could only have occurred if his Pebble had collided with something. But what? He must have traveled a great distance from the prison already. Could it possibly be a piece of wreckage? The Pebble's rotation has slowed considerably. His wrist throbs like the fires of Ruma, but there is no numbness in his fingers, a good sign. He licks his cracked lips. The Pebble's water ampule has miraculously survived the chaos, but he can only access it by removing his helmet. That would be a death sentence.

Only one option presents itself: Wait and hope. Hope at least one of the rebel ships survived the chaotic battle. Hope that a commander took the initiative to search the remains of the asteroid for any sign of the convict whom they were sent to retrieve. But with every minute that passes, he travels farther and farther from any region where rebel ships would search for survivors. Every moment, a sliver of hope escapes him, finding its way out the breach in the wall... until a series of vibrations cause him to crane his head and peer through the hole into space.

Small objects are colliding awkwardly with his Pebble. If they are asteroids, they are like none he has ever seen—all generally the same size and oddly proportioned if they are space rocks. Derek squints, but he can make out no additional details in the darkness. The only light comes from the dim, independently-powered, fluorescent tubes in the interior of his cell. Half of them are dark, too.

Derek detaches one of these tubes, carefully leads it through the hole, and then releases it. He recoils immediately. Corpses. Scores of them, scattered, bloated, floating silently. His heart thunders in his chest, and a chill expands beneath his flesh.

From the prison? No... no, of course not. The prison facility had numbered no more than a few hundred occupants, and rebel warships can hold only dozens. There are too many bodies, too far away. These are the remains of something worse. But corpses mean wreckage. Wreckage might yield supplies. And supplies may mean the difference between survival and becoming another unidentifiable body drifting through the cosmos. Then again, supplies run out. If he cannot make contact with someone soon, Derek doesn't foresee any future for himself other than prolonged death. No one tells tales of men consigned to oblivion.

Derek breathes deeply and peers again at the hellish scene. His glowing tube reveals repulsively deformed bodies. All of them appear to be in civilian clothing. All of them. No sign that they were miners or soldiers. And then he notices the smaller bodies. Children. He imagines their faces—frozen in fear or anguish or perhaps simply confusion. The innocent dead.

Dammit.

In a moment, they all disappear, cloaked again in a veil of darkness. As the Pebble continues on its uncertain trajectory, Derek wrestles with the images he has seen. Has he conjured up these images himself? Has he actually gone mad. The uncertainty terrifies him.

Then a glint of something in the distance. Derek's eyes widen. There it is! Is that a beam of light? And there is another! And another! Five, ten, twenty, fifty! As his cell passes by, the object appears to awaken like a sleeping giant in an Asteri folktale.

It is a ship, a massive one, unfamiliar. The great metal hulk isn't Kumarri, and it is too large to be an Asterisk cruiser. Could it be a marauder spacecraft? No, construction of such a behemoth would be far too expensive. Mining ships don't pass by the outskirts of the Swyre Cluster anymore, instead competing in the ice-rich Innercluster. No trade routes are anywhere nearby. Nothing but dust. Dust and bodies.

Derek's face grows grim. He has a decision to make. In moments, his Pebble will spiral away. He can risk it all and try to reach the ship... or remain in the confines of his cell. There is no choice.

Derek grabs another fluorescent tube, instinctively holds his breath, pushes off a cell wall and propels himself into space. For a split second, he worries his protective clothing will snag on a piece of twisted metal, but his exit is smooth. He is traveling on momentum only. Momentum and desperation. He dreads what he will encounter, and his fears are quickly realized. The lights of the vessel outline a forest of corpses. As he sails toward the dead, a sour taste creeps up the back of his throat. He silently gives thanks for his nutritional injections—he doesn't want the contents of his stomach obscuring his view.

Bodies drift on all sides, bumping and sliding past each other. Derek has difficulty registering the fact that all of these horrors were once living and breathing. Now they are bloated from the water that vaporized within them, blue from lack of oxygen, seared and charred by cosmic radiation, the moisture in their eyes boiled away, leaving a frozen white goop.

He fumbles forward into the carnage, forcing himself to grab hold of a frozen leg to continue his movement toward the ship. The victim's face is cracked and blackened. Around his neck floats a shaggy silver mane. Derek's mind whirls as a realization dawns: the dead aren't Human... or Swyriak... or Kumarri. They are Arketai, the most secretive of the Six Races, resented by nearly all for their neutrality during the Interplanetary War. Pursuing peace left them with the fewest casualties. But now? Has the resentment turned to revenge? Has a fanatic finally lashed out at the nonviolent race? And what are the Arketai doing here? They haven't been seen in this part of the sector for centuries. It makes no sense.

He finds himself thinking back to his childhood. His father had been a playwright and actor; it was from him that Derek had inherited a glibness of tongue. The man eventually gave up the profession for a more stable career as an oxy merchant. Once, only once, he had cast young Derek as an imp who taunted the protagonist. The little rhyme echoes through his mind: *If tossed adrift, blow out not in, or your lungs will burst and your head will spin.* Derek exhales as the dead drift around him.

As he closes the distance to the ship, Derek notices a sort of elegance in its design, almost as if it were created organically. It hovers at a slight upward angle relative to Derek, and has a subtle, but recognizable rotation. The ships lights are blinking now. As it continually turns, a horrible truth is slowly revealed, disappearing and reappearing in the light. Derek's heart drops. The hull appears to be sliced open. Hundreds of grotesque corpses crowd the open wound, like oozing blood. From afar, the vessel had looked active and deadly. But now his mind begins to register that the monstrous craft before him was the *victim*. Dead. What kind of weapon could do that? None that he has seen. He is numb, as he floats toward a cosmic graveyard.

A shred of hope remains. The lights are on. Somebody seems to be home. But are they friend... a blackened head spirals past, still connected to part of the spine... or foe?

Moments later, he slams into the hull with more force that he had intended. Derek loses his grip on the light tube and strains to find purchase among the rivulets of metal. His overgrown fingernails crack and snap amid the effort until he grabs what seems to be a loosened panel. Had it simply been damaged in the battle, or was it an intentional design?

His thoughts veer into his past once more, to his teenage years, when he would watch great ships return to Asterport, often damaged in battle. Asterport was a flurry of activity. Merchants, convoys, messengers, miners. Ships of every size and shape—from nearly every inhabited location in the System—docked at Axle, a masterwork of Asteri engineering and a prominent display of power that was also designed to serve as a deterrent to attacks. In his youth, Derek had hoped to become one of the Nraja, a Kumarri word meaning mechanic, more or less. While wounded soldiers would pour out of a vessel, these men and women in white jumpsuits would rush in. They would crowd a ship's hull, peel back circular panels, and perform microsurgery on a macro patient.

Their job description was simple... and incredibly dangerous. The bravest of the Nraja would wriggle through constricted passageways, deep into the bowels of the ship, toward its energy core. An explosion might be possible at any moment, which could cripple a civilization. Essential crops from the Kumarri and ice from the Swyriak would be unable to reach desperate citizens. And the Nraja would die first. But, yes, one could simply call them mechanics.

But at that age, Derek had hoped to become one. His mother was quick to discourage him. "Heroes and fools tread a similar path," she had said. So he opted for a considerably less heroic occupation in the Asteri government. *Fools indeed*, he thinks as another explosion of pain shoots down his arm. The tips of his fingers have lost all feeling now. He misses Asterport.

Derek examines the panel. Is this a primitive version of one of the cavities that the Nraja utilized back home? There is only one way to find out. He jams his fingers underneath the panel, ignoring the pain, and pries it open. A dark shaft greets him. His palms begin to ache from clinging to the ship's exterior. He curses, and a thin line of spittle dribbles down his chin. He starts to wipe it with his hand and only then remembers the invisible shell around his head. He sighs and plunges into the shadow.

Immersed in darkness, save for a faint red light emanating from somewhere deep within the vessel, he works his way forward. An icy sheen coats the tunnel walls—cold to the touch, even with the invisible barrier protecting his hands. Or is that his imagination? The way begins to slant downward, narrowing as it does, so that Derek's shoulders rub against the metal walls. The confinement reminds him briefly of his time in the Pebble, but in the cell he could do nothing. A bead of sweat trickles from his brow. Here... here he could push on.

Derek grunts, licking the salty sweat trapped in the hair above his lip, inching forward... and suddenly the passage opens up. He floats past a series of exposed rooms in the blinking light, each containing a gruesome scene. A mess hall where metal trays and corpses twirl as if in some sort of Asteri sky-dance. A couple locked in eternal embrace in what used to be living quarters. He gasps. A nursery. A damned nursery. There is no life to be found.

Derek grabs hold of a thin column to stop his movement and steady his nerves. A sealed steel hatch, apparently undamaged, is nearly concealed behind a floating junk pile. He clears the obstruction with his feet. The door bears a metal wheel, similar to the mechanism that had opened and closed his Pebble. At first it is stiff and unyielding, but soon it reluctantly turns, revealing a room that is not what Derek expected. Small, no larger than a supply closet. Empty, useless. With his peripheral vision, he notices the door slowly shutting behind him. He cannot reach it in time. Suddenly, he feels the tug of his body toward the floor—artificial gravity, a sensation he hasn't experienced for quite some time—and he falls to his knees. Frantic, he fumbles around for an exit. This is no place to die, on his knees, separated from the rest of a wounded ship, cut off from even a glimpse of the cosmos.

Click. A panel slides open in front of him. The sound startles him so much that he nearly falls face-first into whatever lies beyond the secret door. Sound? He hasn't heard a noise since his time in the cell, back when the prison was still intact. Sound means there is oxygen. The elaborate door, the panel, the oxygen—Derek has stumbled upon an airlock. An airlock inside the ship! The Arketai certainly prepared for the worst.

He hesitates for only a moment before pressing the button that collapses his headshell into the collar of his suit. The air is thin, but breathable. Buttons and switches line the walls, some still flickering. The area has been left in disarray—discarded papers, equipment, personal belongings. But he is instantly drawn to what stands in the room's center, a brilliant, orange energy core crackling with power just barely contained, power designed to last generations. The vessel—if not its inhabitants —had been fortunate. If, during the conflict, a projectile had so much as grazed the core, the entire ship would have disintegrated in the blink of an eye.

As Derek gazes into the writhing coils of energy, he swears he sees his own demise written within. Then another noise pulls him from his reflections, energizing him and petrifying him simultaneously. It drifts down a corridor leading from the room—a low, monotone voice.

¤

It is too muffled to make out, and there are long pauses, but he is certain it is a male voice. And not far. A lone survivor? A search crew? Aggressors come to finish the job? He recalls a verse from the *Rumalacon*...

> And Ruma spoke, "Let all who carry inside them good intent stand beside My throne, lest all of man fall prey to the whispers in the dark."

Derek's eyes dart back to the pulsing pillar in the middle of the room. Again, there really is no choice. An encounter with another person, whoever they are, increases his likelihood of survival—and his ability to maintain his sanity. He pulls free a damaged pipe that dangles above one of the control boards and weighs it in his hand. It'll do. The voice seems to come from an open passageway at the other end of the room. As he creeps toward the whispers in the dark, he catches another snippet of the incomprehensible call. He turns a corner, and the flickering lights catch on his makeshift weapon, causing it to gleam. Memories of his days facing off against the Swyriak Legion flood his mind. He has killed to defend himself. Many times. If necessary, he can do it again.

The corridor stops abruptly at a door slightly ajar. Although the words printed above it are unfamiliar, he knows a captain's quarters when he sees one. Years ago, a lifetime ago, his first experience with space travel had been rather uneventful. During the two-day journey, he was only an observer, tasked with studying how government officials conducted themselves. The portly, red-haired man who served as captain—*what was his name?*—had allowed him to linger around his quarters and aid him in his paperwork under the condition that he asked only vital questions. And stayed out of trouble. Derek half expects to see the man walk out now and greet him, as he once again hears the voice reverberate, calm and repetitive. Does the room's occupant sense his presence? He breathes deeply before slowly opening the door.

He is shivering immediately, each breath turned to frost. The room is covered in an icy sheen similar to the tunnel he had used to enter the ship, though his gauges still detect oxygen. Perhaps an air coolant pipe was dislodged in the battle? It is a dark room, illuminated by only a single shaft of light coming from somewhere above. What Derek sees beneath that light sends his heart leaping into his throat. A figure sits at a desk, slouched in his chair, staring at the ceiling. He appears deep in thought. Golden ribbon is woven uniformly from the top of his head to the nape of his neck throughout his long silver mane. He betrays no emotion when Derek enters, moving not at all. Derek turns to shut the door behind him. This Arketai officer is not going to run off. It is time for answers.

"I am First Captain Marut Agnem of the Celorn Relocation Fleet. State your purpose here."

Derek whirls around. He speaks in Old Swyrak, a dying language that Derek knows well enough. The captain has yet to lock eyes, keeping remarkably still.

"I am..." For a moment, Derek nearly forgets his name. "I am Derek Dugall, a survivor of the recent conflict at the prison on Nerro Alpha."

No response from the captain, who remains fixated on a severed duct that hangs precariously above him. The rest of the broken pipe rests on the floor.

Derek inches forward. "Are you a survivor as well?"

Again, no reply.

"Are there others? Escape pods?"

Silence.

Derek strides forward, fists clenched. "Listen to me, dammit! Listen to me! I need—"

"I am First Captain Marut Agnem of the Celorn Relocation Fleet. State your purpose here."

Derek is taken aback. Is it a trick of the light? Has exhaustion overcome him? He could swear the captain's lips haven't moved in the slightest, not so much as a quiver. It is said that the reclusive Arketai possess abilities beyond the understanding of the other five races, but he is certain that telepathy is not among them.

He moves closer. "I know. You already said that." And then a terrible thought.

He places a hand on the Arketai's shoulder and recoils in shock. The flesh is as hard as stone. Gritting his teeth, Derek jerks the chair back. The captain slumps to the floor, lifeless, his brittle bones cracking with the fall. His eyes are pits, long extinguished embers. Dried blood has clotted in the left side of his silver mane. His mouth is frozen in an end-of-days smile.

"I am First Captain Marut Agnem of the Celorn Relocation Fleet. State your purpose here."

Derek's sanity recedes each time the audio file loops—the captain's final request. The same fifteen words. Again. And again. And again. And again. And again. The captain continues to stare up at him, his dead eyes suddenly accusatory. *State your purpose here... State your purpose here...*

His head spins, and again he falls to his knees. Tears stream down his cheeks. Now it all adds up—the Arketai in this sector, the advanced weaponry, the civilian bodies, *Celorn Relocation Fleet*. Derek's mind flashes through the tiny corpses floating in the nursery, the Warden's malevolent grin, the captain's lifeless smile, the *Rumalacon* floating somewhere in the void, indecipherable and unheeded. The seeds of madness have been sown, and he is both gardener and garden. His jaw twitches.

¤

She knits her violet eyebrows. "Who is he?"

"That remains a mystery, admiral. The Human offers no name and bears no identification." The second-in-command scratches his Swyriak upper nose. He smirks. "What we have here... is a myth made real."

Before he can explain, a Human enters the room. Robed in mercenary purple, he is tall and broad, his skin charcoal black, his eyes bright and alert. The man's voice is deep, but reserved. "He claims to be a... revenant, sent by Ruma."

"Ruma? As in the flame god?"

The mercenary gives a curt nod.

The admiral runs four fingers through her hair. "Well, he is clearly mentally unsound."

The Swyriak clears his throat. "I think you will find him a rather convincing character, admiral. Scavengers have reported rumors of life signs in this area for years. Malfunctions, delays, and vanishing heat signatures have prevented any actual discoveries."

"Rumors, not facts. Tall tales move faster than light," says the admiral. "And this Human... a delusional fanatic. I have seen the reenactments. I have heard passages read aloud from the holy texts. All of Ruma's revenants are..."

A scrawny, hunched man stumbles in, escorted by a lithe girl with black stains beneath her eyes. He squints upward at the bright lights that dot the ceiling. His jaw twitches. His most distinguishing feature is the unhealthy color of his skin.

"... cerulean. The revenants in the texts are cerulean." At the mention of revenants, the odd man wanders toward her. She eyes him curiously. "And winged," she adds.

The girl speaks quietly. "He is suffering from severe starvation, a poorly treated broken wrist, oxygen deprivation, and cerebral hypoxia." As if on cue, the hunched man dashes about wildly, touching and sniffing everything he can find. The mercenary nearly strikes him when he tugs on his robes. "His brain has been without a steady source of oxygen for too long," the girl explains.

"How did he get *any* oxygen?" asks the admiral.

"Off the dead," offers the Swyriak. "We saw hundreds of empty air canisters piled around him. Pilfered from the corpses is our best guess."

"What of food?"

"That remains an enigma, admiral. Though I have my suspicions..." The mercenary shuffles his feet. "There were few resources available... but the dead were in no short supply." All eyes turn to the self-proclaimed revenant. He grins up at them, gleefully unaware. The captain shudders. "Take him to the holding cell. Do what you can for him."

The girl glumly nods, and the mercenary salutes, grabbing the blue-skinned survivor by his good wrist and pulling him along.

As the trio departs, the Swyriak hesitates. "Admiral, the ship... the people..."

"Arketai, I am quite aware."

"No, you do not understand. This whole scene, this entire catastrophe... it is a remnant of a time before. Before—"

"You are speaking in riddles."

He shakes his head and searches for words. "It is like a perfectly preserved fossil. Of the Era of Flame, before the star went out. Before the planets imploded. The weapons that were used are much too advanced to exist today. Don't you see? The ship is an Arketai evacuation vessel, but they were much too late. A casualty of war."

"Which war?"

"*The* war," he whispers.

¤

The revenant raps his knuckles on the walls as he wanders the corridors, moving his mouth as if he were speaking. His gait is unsteady, betraying a fraying alliance between body and mind. Each step is an effort.

FATHER TIME'S
FELL HAND

I was born beside my gravestone, on a rocky knoll, on a wind-swept plain. This was a customary affair. My people believe that life must begin and end in chorus, a seamless transition for continuity's sake. My life force is supposed to link back up with my birth when I die—or something to that effect, the process still a mystery to me after so many centuries—so my presence never truly disappears from the annals of history. My life force is a thread, they claim. A thread I tug along with me wherever I go—colonial Massachusetts, medieval Japan, tribal Nepal... My life force must be tattered as hell.

The man takes a moment to crack his knuckles, then reaches to clutch a bottle of wine. With his other hand, he grasps blindly for a glass in the cabinet above. His fingers convulse so violently that it wobbles, falls, and shatters on the floor. He grunts, making a neat pile out of the shards with the scuffed tip of his shoe. He takes a swig directly from the bottle before returning to the typewriter.

I have been called sullen, stern, dispirited. It must be said, witnessing humanity's most seminal victories and profound defeats makes you unavoidably cynical. A nonlinear existence makes it difficult to look forward to much of anything. Uncertainty is empowering, but life without revelation is soul-destroying. And, of course, there is the worst of it—the inability to change the course of human history...

He takes another large gulp of wine.

I long ago lost count of my accents over the endless decades, my ever-shifting native tongue. As a child, I spoke the Castilian of the Spanish Inquisition. As a young thespian, one of Lord Chamberlain's Men, I had the voice of a sixteenth-century Londoner. Then came Jutlandic, Navajo, Sicilian, Punjabi... I may have the order incorrect. I am a traveler who grew to despise many of my destinations. Plague, famine, sewage in the streets... we all have our breaking points. I was glad, in a manner of speaking, to return to the twentieth-century. This time, I was born in Bavaria, just as the Third Reich was raising its ugly head. As a child, I tried to warn my family about the horrors to come. They didn't believe me. Nobody ever believes. Time has no emotion, but this was especially cruel.

The writer pauses once more, crossing and uncrossing his legs, picking at the arms of his chair, scratching his graying beard.

But I had to survive. So that I could die. I had to leave my family to their fate, so that I might dictate my own. It was difficult, but I had to live a long life. I had to cross an ocean. I had to come here, to this house, to this wine cellar, familiar yet so far in my past. I was young, in both age and existence, the last time I lived in this place. I enjoyed my drink. I always do, no matter my circumstances.

He takes quick, periodic glances over his shoulder. He sighs, finally, pushing the return lever and watching the paper readjust itself.

This isn't a damned autobiography—this is a suicide note of the damned. Believe me, I have killed myself too many times to count. But an end to one life has never put an end to my existence. Always another location, another era. But this time, I will die. My existence will be forcibly removed from the timeline. I was once told that time is stubborn like a stream. If you throw a pebble into a stream, the water continues on its way. If you push a boulder into a stream, the water redirects itself. Time self-corrects—that's just the way of it. Time cannot be intentionally changed. But I believe I have found a way to change MY time.

Pause. The man nudges at the revolver on his desk, taking the opportunity to glance behind him once more.

I don't want my death to unravel the timeline, so this is also a ransom note. I am holding time captive. Probability would suggest that somewhere, sometime, my lifetimes would overlap. Still, my luck is not lost on me. In mere minutes, an earlier incarnation will walk down the cellar steps in search of a fine vintage. I am prepared to fire a bullet into the skull of that version of me. The ripple effect would be unfathomable. I have left my mark on too many eras, touched too much history. He will not... cannot... allow this to occur. And so Father Time himself will be forced to accommodate my wishes. Eliminate my existence. Seal my fate. Or face the consequences—it is your choice, old friend.

One more darting look. One can never be too cautious.

I am writing this so that my plan is set in stone. There is no going back now. I have set things in motion. Waiting for my demise, I think I will recount the words of the Immortal Bard, although in a far different context than what Shakespeare intended. I should know. I witnessed the original performance.

A cruel chill, its origin unidentifiable, makes itself present.

Since brass, nor stone, nor earth, nor boundless sea,
But sad mortality o'ersways their power,
How with this rage shall beauty hold a plea,
Whose action is no stronger than a flower?
O, how shall summer's honey breath hold out
Against the wreckful siege of battering days,

When rocks impregnable are not so stout,
Not gates of steel so strong, but time decays?

The lights flicker, dimming and brightening as if communicating.

When I have seen by Time's fell hand defac'd
The rich-proud cost of outworn buried age;
When sometime lofty towers I see down-ras'd
And brass eternal, slave to mortal rage;
When I have seen the hungry ocean gain
Advantage on the kingdom of the shore,
And the firm soil of the wat'ry main,
Increasing store with loss and loss with store;

The air is filled with a dull humming.

When I have seen such interchange of state,
Or state itself confounded to decay;
Ruin hath taught me thus ruminate—
That Time will come and take my love away.

The room and all within begin to warp and twist.

This thought is as death, which cannot choose
But weep to have that which it fears to lose.

Darkness. Silence. Stillness. Then, the metallic clang of a typewriter's keys...

He is here. At last.

¤

On a rocky knoll, on a windswept plain, several figures in shabby funeral garments huddle together to escape the frigid cold. As the wind whistles across the surface of the gravestone, the epitaph begins to fade, slowly, inexorably. Moments after the words vanish, new ones are etched with a steady, fell hand:

Neither stone, nor earth, nor boundless sea,
Can overcome or outlast me,
Because the meat in man will wither and rot,
And the blood of life will congeal and clot,
Because flesh will tear and wear and peel,
The mortal man shall assuredly kneel.

The muffled wails of a newborn child can be heard six feet below. They cease swiftly.

DEAD RINGER

The night watchman pads about uncertainly in the dawn's light, a hand pressed against his heaving chest. Surrounding him is an expansive field of golden wheat, its dew glistening in the encroaching sun. His thoughts are darker, occupied by the nearby burial ground, the harrowing sounds he heard the night before...

He sends forth a silent prayer.

The crunch of gravel underfoot. The night watchman swings himself around to face the cemetery that plagues his dreams. A gray stallion makes its way out of the cemetery gates, its steely eyes locked firmly on the road ahead. Douglas Dunbarrow rides atop, wearing only black, a bowler hat resting under his arm as his hands loosely grip the reins. His auburn hair, usually kept tidy, is brushed about by the breeze. His hawk-like face is bookended by fiery sideburns that fall to his neck.

Douglas offers a polite nod. "They've found a new man to watch over the dead, I see."

The watchman speaks between clenched teeth. "What's your business in the cemetery at this early hour?" His gray hair, stringy and matted, flops this way and that as he glances toward the graveyard.

"Paying my respects to a few old friends." Douglas's reply is quick. He senses the watchman's suspicion. "I'm no grave robber, of that I can assure you." A pause. "You may inspect my belongings if you wish."

The watchman bites his lower lip, weighing his options. "That will not be necessary. Move along." Douglas salutes with two fingers, urging his steed into a trot. After a moment, he hears wheezing, as the watchman has rushed up beside him once more. "Hold up, now!"

Douglas slows his horse this time, not halting the animal. He looks upon the night watchman expectantly, and not without a hint of annoyance. "Yes?"

The man clears his throat, searching for words. "Did you hear anything... peculiar in that place?"

Douglas runs his fingers through his auburn mane. "I can't imagine what you mean," he says at last.

"That is to say, unusual noises of any kind?" *As clear as the clock tower at noon. A piercing tempest of the devil's own creation.*

"The wind... plays tricks on you, sir." The stallion is still now. They both turn to face the graveyard, their eyes running across the lichen-draped trees that shroud it from view.

"You don't suppose..." the watchman speaks carefully. "If you were to dig up one of those graves an' peel back the unearthed coffin's lid... You don't suppose you'd be confronted with bloody scratch marks—like in the stories. Splintered fingernails, a rotting corpse upright, its eyes open..."

Douglas reaches down to pat the man on the shoulder, releasing a forced laugh. "Nonsense, though I applaud your creativity. Sound is distorted." He taps his temples. "Minds make mistakes. Perhaps you require some rest." Douglas blinks away his own exhaustion. "Best we all get some rest 'n' peace, hmm?"

The watchman is left in a cloud of upturned dust, pondering their conversation and watching the stark contrast of the rider's long black overcoat as his shrinking horse sails through a sea of endless wheat.

¤

The dead man's glass eye is unsettling, its green iris an oasis in a desert of rotting, gray flesh. The mortician would have closed the eyelids, but he always felt more confident with a constant reminder of the cadaver's lifeless state. If the tales are to be believed, muffled howls of those long thought dead may still be heard, suffocating in the darkness six feet under. That cannot be allowed to happen under his care. After all, the mortician has to preserve his reputation along with the bodies—the two tasks are not unrelated. One mistake is all it takes to end a career in his profession. So he finds the confirmation of death comforting.

Of course, precautions still have to be taken. For a moment, he turns his attention to the coffin that will soon house the body. It has become a popular practice—installing a bell beside the grave with a string tied to the corpse's finger. *Paranoia. That's what it is*, the mortician thinks. *Dead men are dead men.*

He waves away a fly, returning to the cadaver to trim the man's whiskers and apply cosmetics to his sunken cheeks. After an hour, he steps back, inspecting his work. He shuts the eyelids with care, admiring his illusion. He *is* good. The face glows warmly, though no blood flows. The smell of decomposing tissue is masked behind a blockade of honey and cinnamon. The lips contort in a manufactured smile. As do the mortician's. A dead man lives again.

¤

It is a meager funeral procession. The deceased's sister-in-law, her gaze locked on her fading boots. The single son, his unruly auburn hair kept at bay beneath a bowler hat. And the priest, the trim of his sagging robe growing soggy as it drags across the cemetery's morning dew.

"... I heard the voice of the fourth living creature saying, 'Come.' I looked, and behold, an ashen horse..." Douglas glances at his grieving aunt, watching as teardrops form at the corners of her eyes. He is stoic, his mouth a grim line. *There is no misery in death.* He has heard many firsthand accounts.

"... and he who sat on it had the name Death; and Hades was following with him..." *What a sorry affair this is,* Douglas muses, absentmindedly fingering the pipe in his pocket. *How we dress a man up, parade his decaying corpse about. Fly food, that's all* corpses are. Now the soul... that is a different matter entirely. It is not the body that anchors the soul, nor the coffin or tombstone.

"... Authority was given to them over a fourth of the earth, to kill with sword and with famine and with pestilence and by the wild beasts of the earth..." *And liquor,* Douglas silently adds. A memory surfaces...

The farmer mowed down the grain indiscriminately, twirling in the fields like a madman, scythe in hand. A wide grin adorned his face. A crazed grin. Although random, his movements had a certain rhythm about them, an intricate ritual only the farmer understood. Yellow stalks took to the air, assisted by the swinging blade and assailed by soil upturned in the man's dance. No more troubles. No more worries. Just raw devastation. A reaping...

"Father?" The man stopped short, letting the scythe fall to his side. His salt-and-pepper whiskers quivered. "Father?"

He turned tentatively. Swallowed. "Douglas..."

"What are you—Father, why are you out here?"

The man's green glass eye glinted in the moonlight. His breath smelled like cheap whiskey. "Preparing for the harvest, that is all."

Douglas frowned. "It is cold, Father. You should come inside."

The man knelt in front of his son, tussling the boy's fiery hair. "Of course, of course. Let's... go inside."

"Father—" The man draped an arm over the boy's shoulder, wielding the scythe with the other. White knuckles gripped the shaft. The pair ambled toward the farmhouse, despite the bitter frost. The imprints of their feet disappeared in the snowdrift behind them.

The priest flips several pages forward and reads a few more verses. Finally, he shuts his tattered Bible, raising his arms to the misty heavens. The next passage he recites from memory. "So the angel thrust his sickle into the earth and gathered the vine of the earth, and threw it into the great winepress of the wrath of God. And the winepress was trampled outside the city, and blood came out of the winepress, up to the horses' bridles…"

¤

The stonecutter prefers to cloak his shop in darkness when he is at work. Heavy violet curtains are drawn, all but a few candle wicks pinched. When Douglas silently opens the door, a shaft of golden sunlight barrages the workshop. After shutting the door behind him, Douglas tucks his bowler hat under his arm and loosens his scarf.

There is movement in the room's far corner. Perhaps it comes from behind the slabs of granite leaning against the far wall. Or from within the maze of statues in varying states of completion—angels and aristocrats, gods and gargoyles. But no, the noise emanates from a wooden hatch, creaky with age. Out of it emerges the stonecutter, his calloused hands feeling about for a handhold. Eventually, he hoists himself up. He had been strong in his youth, but the man's gait is unsteady and his back is stooped. His eyes squint behind copper spectacles. "Mr. Dunbarrow, is that you?" He shambles forward.

"It is."

The stonecutter looks at him curiously. "I must admit, it is an uncommon thing to have visitors during work hours."

"My apologies then, I prefer not to be disturbed at work either. I was hoping to inquire about a certain project of yours."

"Ah, the—ahem—the gravestone of yours. The... unique request." The man motions for Douglas to wait where he is, turning to descend back down through the hatch. Biding his time, Douglas wanders through the workshop, observing silently the statues within. The frozen figures grope and grasp as if trapped in the stone's embrace. Like half-unearthed fossils seeing the light of day after a millennia of darkness.

"Eerie, are they not?"

Douglas whips around, his hat tumbling out of his fingers.

The stonecutter stands, transfixed by his creations. He holds a large object wrapped in cloth. "The unfinished ones, I mean." He hobbles toward the nearest of these—a girl, the features of her face undefined. "Do you know, Mr. Dunbarrow, what Michelangelo once said?"

Douglas kneels slowly, retrieving his hat and wiping away the dust. "I imagine he said a great many things."

"He said 'Every block of stone has a statue inside it, and it is the task of the sculptor to discover it.'" The stonecutter turns to Douglas. "He could not have been closer to the truth." With a grunt, the man sets the heavy bundle on a table and begins to unwrap the gravestone within.

"Do you know what humanity's great illusion is, Mr. Dunbarrow?"

This time, Douglas declines to answer.

"We use the phrase 'set in stone' to describe things unchanging..." The stonecutter flips the gravestone around to reveal a distinct lack of any engraving at all. It is blank. "Nothing is set in stone, Mr. Dunbarrow. The world wears away all things."

Douglas examines the man's work, nodding in satisfaction. "Payment?"

"No need. I suspect this will not be our last transaction."

¤

"I don't much like funerals. I feel safer when the Lord isn't paying attention." The stallion meanders through the weeds that grow around the headstones. The moonlight glimmers upon the moss-covered trees that surround the cemetery, creating a dappled pattern on the horse's ashen coat. The rider wears funeral garments—a black bowler hat and overcoat. The whistling wind causes his scarf to billow behind him like a hastily hoisted flag. The man dismounts, tying his stallion to one of the trees.

He continues to speak. "Which is odd, in a way, seeing how much of my time is spent in the graveyard. But the Lord doesn't approve of that either. Father certainly wouldn't. Talking to spirits isn't something I imagine much of anyone approves of, in fact." He eyes the graves. "You people understand."

The man removes his hat, placing it delicately on a stone cross. This gravestone is older than most, protruding from the dry soil at an awkward angle, cracked in places, transformed by cascading ivy and withered ferns. The epitaph is illegible. "Hope you don't mind, Carolyn." He smiles and reaches into a pack atop his horse. "This time, you can choose the words." He sets down the unmarked slab.

Douglas Dunbarrow strolls along the row of graves with his hands in his pockets, humming a children's tune and kicking at pebbles. Though small in stature, he carries himself like a general standing before his troops before sending them into battle.

Douglas climbs a grassy knoll, taking a seat on a tombstone at the graveyard's edge. For a moment, he is still, admiring the briefly illuminated clouds as they pass before the moon. Then he draws a pipe from the pocket of his overcoat, lighting it with the ease of a practiced hand. After a few graceful puffs, he sends the smoke skyward. It swirls into nothingness.

He returns the pipe to its place. In its stead, a brass baton finds its way into his grasp, his thin fingers coiling around it like a snake on a tree branch. Three times he taps the tombstone. Standing now, he raises his arms to the heavens.

"Shall we begin?"

The air is still for a moment, then erupts in a chorus of bells and the neighs of a bewildered horse.

ON THE DOT

T he waiter in the cafe on the corner of Spruce and Wells had been sneezing for four years. His scrunched nose retreated into his face, its bridge webbed with wrinkles. His half-closed eyes were yellow crescents. His mouth was agape, tongue unfurled in a perpetual "ahh." For months, Martin had found himself passing the cafe, awaiting with some impatience the resolution, the closure that could only be provided by that final, elusive "choo."

And yet the waiter's face remained contorted, its muscles drawn taut like a small glove forced over the knuckles of a meaty hand, the prospect of release still a distant notion. Martin's jaw clenched at the very thought.

The tray that perched precariously on the fingertips of the waiter's left hand was tilted at an angle that should have spelled disaster, had time been cooperating. Instead, the water that sloshed out of the glasses sat suspended in the air, liquid sculptures fixed in place and glittering in the orange light of the setting sun.

Martin no longer meandered awestruck across this eerie stillness. His chest no longer tightened at the pressure of this oppressive silence. He was no longer cognizant of every crunch of gravel underfoot, every shuddering breath that escaped his lungs. Martin even found some refuge in slumber, despite the stubborn constant that was the ever-present sun locked in the sky. After months trapped in this purgatory, the miraculous had become the mundane.

Martin crossed the street. The truck still stalled at the stop sign; the beat-up blue Ford's twisting exhaust was a rigid, accusatory finger. Martin stuffed his hands in his pockets and stared up at the forbidding red octagon. He adjusted his wedding ring. Then he shook his head and carried on his way.

A 'V' of geese hovered above, a familiar arrow urging him onward. Martin liked to imagine that the birds were hanging from invisible strings, components of a heavenly baby mobile. He continued to muse on this image as he retrieved an apple from the base of a street vendor's pyramid. Martin sighed. Disturbing the foundation of the pile had no effect; the fruit floated without support.

Apple juice dribbled down his chin, and he wiped it off with his hand. Martin cupped the sticky pulp in his palm, examining it as if for the first time. His touch allowed an object to exist at a faster frame of reference, a fact that never ceased to amaze him. Martin frowned. If only the same happened when he attempted to interact with people. He missed conversation, camaraderie. His lip now curled at the static features of the townspeople. Unresponsive neighbors... Frozen friends... Hannah... Martin stopped himself as his lip began to quiver.

He attempted to distract himself by scanning his surroundings, even though he had committed every time-locked denizen to memory. Martin spotted the familiar boy on a bicycle, sweat glistening off the boy's brow, his cheeks crimson. He held a rolled newspaper aloft, brandishing it like a sword. A newspaper boy?

Martin thought they had disappeared along with milkmen and fax machines. Then again, he had also thought that time was inexorable.

Martin noted the date immortalized in tiny black letters on the corner of the newspaper. February 29. Always the 29th of February. An ugly day, Martin decided. The necessary consequence of a leap year, and yet the date reeked of lingering incorrectness. A misprint's day in the sun. And by some misstep in time's endless march, Martin was fated to call the 29th his personal eternity.

Then he noticed the fly on the bicycle's handlebar, the bug that the boy was winding up to swat. In the early days, Martin had been transfixed by creatures of the air. How callously speed concealed beauty in plain sight – hidden behind the blur of a hummingbird, behind the beating of a moth's wings, or, in a case close to his heart, behind the buzz of a certain black-and-yellow pollinator. It had taken several months for Martin to suspect that time had slowed, not stopped. But how to confirm this hunch? Then Martin had discovered the bumblebee hovering an inch above the railing on his balcony. Without wasting any time (though Martin had plenty to spare), he had marked a small 'X' in white chalk below the insect that seemingly had been rendered motionless.

He returned to the balcony periodically. At first he thought it wishful thinking. After nearly a year had passed, he was certain. The bee no longer hovered directly above the chalk 'X.'

Time still flowed! But the stream had been reduced to a barely perceptible trickle.

That bee reignited hope. A chance to be forgiven.

His eyes left the fly on the bicycle's handlebar and returned briefly to the boy's newspaper. Martin made a silent vow. The day he escaped this would be the last day he ever swatted an insect. He owed them that much.

He shivered, then left the bicyclist behind. His next stop was another piece of the daily ritual. Martin exited the flower shop a minute later, five quarters lighter and a tulip in hand. He made certain to pay each time. Impossibly tall stacks of coins lined the edge of the counter now; the florist would find in an instant that she was surrounded by great metallic walls.

Only one destination remained. The location that stood as a testament to his failure. The place that, on each visit, drove him to tears. And yet he returned. Why? Sometimes Martin asked himself that question.

Martin still remembered what he had told her over the phone. What he had promised her. *I'll be there. Ballerini's at six o'clock. On the dot, baby. On the dot.* Martin inhaled sharply, trying and failing to dispel the unpleasant memory that followed.

But how could he forget? The blaring telephone in his cubicle startling him awake. The sheer panic after a glance at the clock on the wall told him it was 5:59. In a jolt of fear and shame, the world seemed to freeze around him. Then it stayed frozen.

And then the long wait. Hours spent staring at the minute hand, willing it onward. The same minute. Four years.

Martin slowed his pace as the green awning came into view. And the white lettering: BALLERINI'S ON THE LAKE. Dragging his feet on the pavement, he forced himself to the doorframe. At this point, he knew what to expect. She would be sitting at the table in the corner, the one with the candelabra and the frozen flames. She was always there, hands resting gently in her lap, eyes looking down at her menu. And always that earnest half-smile.

But those eyes were always vacant, her smile just a passing moment. The ritual would continue. He would kiss her cheek, shed a tear. Then he would sigh, turn his back, and toss the flower into the lake, where it would join hundreds of others. A pool of a thousand petals. Then he would shuffle home, find some way to fall asleep. Why should today be any different?

Martin closed his eyes and stepped through the threshold. But this time...

The noise that greets him sends him stumbling over his own feet. Clinking china. Hushed conversation. The wailing of a baby. He crashes into a wandering patron.

"Whoa, whoa, you alright, bud?"

"What... what—" Martin almost vomits. "What time is it?"

The man eyes him curiously, then squints at his wristwatch. "Uh... six. On the dot."

Martin gasps. "Thank you! Oh thank you!" He envelops the man in a bear hug.

"Don't mention it..." says the befuddled patron to no one in particular. Martin has long since pushed past him.

Martin races across the room, dodging waiters and diners, baskets of bread and platters of pasta. The corner... the corner... there it is.

She doesn't look up as he runs up, panting. "You made it. What do you think, fettuccine alfredo or the gah-nochi? Gah-nocchi? Gnocchi!" She looks up and grins. "Hey, is that a flower?"

Martin returns the smile. "Hannah, happy anniversary."